PRAISE FOR SCARECROW

"A stellar collection that runs the gamut of Urban Fantasy to Weird Fiction. Easily the most consistently satisfying anthology I've read in years."
— K.L. Young, Executive Editor, *Strange Aeons Magazine*

"With fifteen talented writers and a subject that is both evocative and memorable, Rhonda Parrish's new anthology, *Scarecrow*, is no straw man. Like any good scarecrow, this anthology is truly outstanding in its field. Don't be scared to pick this up and give it a read."
— Steve Vernon, author of *Tatterdemon*

PRAISE FOR THE SERIES:
RHONDA PARRISH'S MAGICAL MENAGERIES

FAE

"A delightfully refreshing collection that offers a totally different take on your usual fairy stories! I should have known that editor Parrish (who also edits the cutting edge horror zine, *Niteblade*) would want to offer something quite unique. I found it difficult to stop reading as one story ended and another began—all fantastic work by gifted writers. Not for the faint of heart, by any means."
— Multiple Bram Stoker® winner, Marge Simon

"Anyone with an abiding love of Faerie and the Folk who dwell there will find stories to enjoy in *FAE*."
— Tangent

"There's no Disney-esque flutter and glitter to be found here—but there are chills and thrills aplenty."
— Mike Allen, author of *Unseaming,* editor of *Clockwork Phoenix*

"Nibble on this deliciously wondrous collection of stories of fae one at a time or binge on its delights on one night, you'll love the faerie feast this collection provides. Love, loss, horror, healing, humor, tragedy--it's all here, where stories of magical beings and the humans they encounter will enthrall and enlighten the reader about both the mundane and the otherworldly. I devoured it."
— Kate Wolford, editor of *Beyond the Glass Slipper*, editor and publisher of *Enchanted Conversation: A Fairy Tale Magazine.*

CORVIDAE

"Smart and dark like the corvids themselves, this excellent collection of stories and poems will bring you a murder of chills, a tiding of intrigue, a band of the fantastic, and—most of all—an unkindness of sleepy mornings after you've stayed up too late reading it!"
— Karen Dudley, author of *Kraken Bake*

"Corvidae evokes the majesty and mischief of corvid mythologies worldwide—and beyond our world—in a collection that is fresh and thoroughly enjoyable."
— Beth Cato, author of *The Clockwork Dagger*

"Magic and corvids collide in this certain to intrigue anthology."
— Joshua Klein, hacker and inventor of the crow vending machine

"A creepy, crazy kaleidoscope of corvids. Nothing short of a thrill ride when this anthology takes flight."
— Susan G. Friedman, Ph. D., Utah State University; behaviorworks.org.

"As sparkling and varied as a corvid's hoard of treasures, *Corvidae* is by turns playful and somber, menacing and mischievous. From fairy tale to steampunk adventure, from field of war to scene of crime, these magical birds will take you to places beyond your wildest imaginings."

— Jennifer Crow, poet and corvid-by-marriage

Titles in the Anthology Series
Rhonda Parrish's Magical Menageries

Fae
Corvidae
Scarecrow
Sirens (coming 2016)

Scarecrow

Edited by
RHONDA PARRISH

Rhonda Parrish's Magical Menageries
Volume Three

WORLD WEAVER PRESS

Published by World Weaver Press
Alpena, Michigan
www.WorldWeaverPress.com

Cover designed by Eileen Wiedbrauk of World Weaver Press.
Cover photo: "Red Corn" Copyright © 2014 by Dan Wiedbrauk of One Candle
Photos, one-candle.com.

First Edition: August 2015

ISBN: 0692430229
ISBN-13: 978-0692430224

Also available as an ebook.

CONTENTS

INTRODUCTION
Rhonda Parrish – 7

SCARECROW HANGS
Jane Yolen – 9

KAKASHI & CROW
Megan Fennell – 10

THE ROOFNIGHT
Amanda C. Davis – 30

SKIN MAP
Kim Goldberg – 43

A FIST FULL OF STRAW
Kristina Wojtaszek – 46

JUDGE & JURY
Laura VanArendonk Baugh – 54

WAKING FROM HIS MASTER'S DREAM
Katherine Marzinsky – 78

THE STRAW SAMURAI
Andrew Bud Adams – 90

BLACK BIRDS
Laura Blackwood – 110

EDITH AND I
Virginia Carraway Stark – 118

SCARECROW PROGRESSIONS
(RUBBER DUCK REMIX)
Sara Puls – 123

TRUTH ABOUT CROWS
Craig Pay – 134

TWO STEPS FORWARD
Holly Schofield – 146

ONLY THE LAND REMEMBERS
Amanda Block – 153

IF I ONLY HAD AN AUTOGENIC COGNITIVE DECISION MATRIX
Scott Burtness – 175

CONTRIBUTORS
184

ANTHOLOGIST
189

RHONDA PARRISH'S MAGICAL MENAGERIES

MORE GREAT SHORT FICTION

SCARECROW

INTRODUCTION

So that there will be no debate, let me be perfectly clear—*Corvidae* came first.

I am a bird person, and corvids are among my favourites. I love them so much, in fact, that I have them tattooed, permanently etched, onto my body. So the idea for *Corvidae* came first; but scarecrow stories are such a perfect complement to corvids that *Scarecrow* was conceived soon after.

Ever since I first watched *The Wizard of Oz*, I've been intrigued by scarecrows but, unfortunately, I don't actually know any. So while I was able to ask my friend, Magnus E. Magpie, who usually haunts Twitter as the magpie personality @YegMagpie, to offer Tweet-length "cawmentary" on the stories in *Corvidae*, I didn't know a straw man who could do the same for this book.

Magnus is a brave bird, however, so despite sending me emails which said things like, "Am steeling myself with a slightly stepped-on breakfast sandwich to read the scarecrow [book] . . . gulp!" he's offering a bird's perspective on these stories as well. I'm delighted to share his bird's eye view online at worldweaverpress.com/scarecrow.html as well as on my own website rhondaparrish.com.

Magnus had every right to be nervous about reading a scarecrow anthology, and not just because he's a bird. Most scarecrow fiction I've encountered has been rather dark: "The Family of Blood" in Doctor Who, *Feathertop* and Steve Vernon's *Tatterdemon* just to name a few. The scarecrows in those stories are all either evil, doomed or both—but

I never envisioned this as a horror anthology. I wanted darkness but I wanted light as well.

I've been blown away by the creativity the authors within these pages have shown. They've given this anthology fantastic depth and range.

Scarecrow covers a wide range of genres from urban fantasy ("Kakashi and Crow") to the re-telling of an Asian fairy tale ("The Straw Samurai"), science fiction ("If I Only Had an Autogenic Cognitive Decision Matrix") to romance ("A Fist Full of Straw"). The voices of the stories are varied as well—the classic tones of "The Roofnight" and lyrical prose in "Skin Map" are but two, there's also distant narration, blunt, dreamy, they're all here but what I love most about this book is the huge variety of scarecrows these authors have created.

We've got scarecrows made of straw, of steel ("Truth About Crows"), imagination ("Waking From His Master's Dream"), memory ("Black Birds") and flesh. They are horrific, empathetic ("Scarecrow Progressions, Rubber Duck Remix"), lonely ("Edith and I") and vengeful. Some created by human hands ("Two Steps Forward"), evolution, or chosen by the draw ("Only the Land Remembers"). Jane Yolen's poem, "Scarecrow Hangs," takes us back to Oz and though it stands on its own, Laura VanArendonk Baugh's story, "Judge & Jury" is the sequel to her *Corvidae* contribution, "Sanctuary."

That is precisely what I'd hoped to accomplish in this anthology: diversity. Diversity in theme, mood, setting, voice, genre . . . and though *Scarecrow* has quite a strong Western Canadian feel to it (which is, admittedly, my home), I think I was successful, and I am incredibly proud.

So yes, *Corvidae* came first, but *Scarecrow* is second to none.

— Rhonda Parrish, Editor

SCARECROW HANGS

Jane Yolen

"[T]he Scarecrow of Conciliation." —Teresa Matlock

He hangs there like some old corn god,
eyeing the furrows, hoping to see
some good old-fashioned humping going on,
anything to bring fertility back into the world.

Waiting on resurrection, that uncertain future,
where we all cavort in long draperies
or twang uncomfortable lyres, he smiles.
He cannot help it. The smile is painted on.

Deep inside that straw head, he remembers
dancing down the rows with a girl, a sulky dog,
an iron man, a large maned cat. A dream,
he thinks. But as with all scarecrows

life is not about living but conciliation—
making the elder gods happy, resolving
crow murders, keeping boys with matches
out of his vicinity, playing it safe.

It is the most human thing about him.

KAKASHI & CROW

Megan Fennell

I knew I was dreaming, but it was a sweet dream so I let it ride.

1907, Ellis Island. The immigrants were streaming off the ships in a weary tide, clutching raggedy suitcases and herding wide-eyed children. Up above, the ocean breeze was my own personal rollercoaster. I was taking unholy pleasure in dive-bombing the whole sorry lot of them as they shuffled along, making the women shriek and the men flap their hats at me. It was the most fun I'd had in weeks, weaving that colorful tapestry of curses in a hundred different languages, flipping and dancing and staying just out of reach. Welcome to the brave new world, suckers! Take a nice deep whiff of your American dream!

There was a loud *rat-a-tat-tat* right next to my head and I jolted awake, jerking away from the noise before my brain sorted out the difference between gunfire and the sound of a billy club being dragged along the bars of a holding cell.

"On your feet, asshole," the guard called through the bars. "Looks like someone out there loves you."

I blinked, bleary-eyed, before the sight of him fully registered. He could have made up for his receding hairline if he wasn't ugly. And he could have made up for being ugly by not being a total dick. Sadly, he didn't seem to be making up for much of anything.

I sat up, rubbing the sore muscles in the back of my neck. A three-toed sloth could count on its fingers how many people in the world loved me, so I didn't get the joke.

"Say again, brother?" I said.

"I ain't your *brudder*," he shot back, forcing an accent about a hundred years out of date. "Some guy up front decided to waste his money. You made bail."

I got to my feet real slow, trying to figure out the trap. I'd been wearing the same name and face in this city long enough that the boys in blue had gotten to know me and they'd set my bail so high I figured I ought to get an engraved nameplate for my cell this time around.

"Does some-guy-up-front have a name?" I shuffled over to the door, standing where I was supposed to stand, keeping my hands in the open. Behaving is easier when someone's unlocking a cage for you.

"I didn't ask your boyfriend his name," he muttered, working the lock. "Tall guy. Asian-looking. Got a bit of a dead-eyed stare going on. Hell, maybe you've got debts to a gang and this guy's about to make my life a whole lot easier and better smelling."

He was still talking, saying something about turning off the security cameras in the parking lot out back, but my spine had turned into one long icicle, fused solid with fear. The door of my cell was wide open and I just stood there, fighting the urge to swing it shut again. *Tall guy. Asian-looking. No way, no way, not after all this time . . .*

A drug-debt to a gang would have been a hell of a lot easier to deal with. I was much older than I looked, and scrappier too, but there was no controlling the stranglehold fear that grabbed onto me at that description. Like thinking you're all alone in a dark room and then hearing someone cough.

Kakashi.

"Move, Johnny," the guard barked, jabbing me with his baton. "Pow-wow your ass on out of there unless you want to stay."

I can't say I was proud of what I did next, but I was stressed and sore and the one person who'd come the closest to putting an end to old Johnny Crow had found me again and, goddamn it, a pow-wow was a *gathering*, not a way of moving. So I locked onto the guard's eyes with mine, letting the old power crackle along the path of my bones, and learned a truth that a part of him knew and a bigger part of him didn't want to. I hooked onto the thought like a prize catch and reeled it to the forefront of his mind.

Funny how Jennie never misses her book club meetings even though she's never really been a reader since you married her. Funny that it always, always falls on the same Thursday as Greg's poker night where he never seems to win or lose any money.

Funny, isn't it?

∿

I strolled my way to freedom with a grimy gray lost-and-found t-shirt wadded against my bleeding nose. The guard packed an admirable right jab. I mean, it didn't make up for having a marriage that was falling apart as fast as his looks, but it was a nice solid punch just the same.

I knew where Kakashi would be waiting even before my eyes found him. Whenever we were within range of each other, the old lines of magic we both carried within us collided with a vicious friction. Flint and tinder, saw-blade and tree trunk, toddler's reaching hand and red-hot stove. I hated how I knew exactly which side of each of those metaphors was me.

He was standing by the sliding door, a creature of perfect stillness in the bustling lobby, like something carved centuries ago. Which, technically, I suppose he was. From this distance, he almost looked human. Neatly put together with black suit and white shirt, he stood just shy of six feet (though he always *felt* taller in my head) and could have passed as a professor coming over from Tokyo. But the illusion fell apart quick when you noticed that his polished-obsidian eyes never blinked, his chest failed to rise and fall under that tidy suit, and that just looking at him made it feel like a parade of ants was marching mercilessly along all the most sensitive parts of you.

Well, maybe that last part was reserved for my kind alone.

I pulled the blood-stained shirt away from my nose and waved it at him with a shit-eating grin. He wouldn't try to fight me here. We never danced in public. Anyway, I hadn't done anything wrong. Lately. To him. That he knew about.

So that made it more like skinny-dipping in a tank full of well-fed piranha, rather than starving ones.

"Kakashi, my brother!" I greeted him. Strolling up to him felt like walking upriver, waist-deep. "Twenty-five years. But I do like your timing."

He inclined his head slightly, his expression moving not at all. "Twenty-three years," he corrected softly. His once-upon-a-time accent had been eaten up by the blank slate nothingness of modern North American. "And we have never been brothers."

"Nobody wants to be poor old Johnny Crow's brother today," I sighed.

He didn't answer, just took his silent measure of me, making me feel like a bug under a magnifying glass. I fidgeted and scratched at the dried blood on the side of my nose, a hundred questions and accusations roiling under my skin. It was a relief when he finally spoke again.

"*Karasu-tengu*," he said, "Do you still speak prophesy?"

I winced, a little at the old name, a little at the question. I would have loved to say no, but I knew damn well his arrival was the reason I'd been dreaming of New York in the years when it really had been 'new.' Those ambitious immigrants swarming ashore had carried more luggage in their hearts than in their suitcases; some families had believed in the kind of scarecrows that packed a bit more clout than the basic straw-stuffed-coveralls, we're-off-to-see-the-wizard affair. They had believed in the power of the Kakashi so deeply that the eastern scarecrow had been able to dig his wooden toes into western soil and throw a monkey wrench into my centuries of undisturbed machinations.

Awful hard to deny that the gift of prophesy was still clinging to me like a stubborn burr when he turned up on the heels of my dream about our meeting place. Well then . . .

"When it suits me," I said.

He nodded, the picture of solemnity. "Then let us leave, unless you would prefer to remain here."

I gave a last resigned swipe of the grubby shirt over my sore nose and stuffed the bundle into my canvas knapsack. Never wise to leave your blood lying around where just anyone could find it.

"It's not so bad here," I said. I headed towards the big sliding doors just the same. "Folk in here tell stories the old way, starting at the end. Every damn one starts 'Here's the story of why it's not my fault.' I miss that sometimes."

Out in the parking lot, I discovered that I'd been cheating myself out of a beautiful summer day while biding my time in custody. The sun was bright and hot in a clear sky and the air had a rich green growing smell to it.

"Is that why you were in prison again?" Kakashi asked. His voice was always so toneless that it was hard to untangle sarcasm from honest curiosity. "Do you come back for the stories?"

I tossed him a reckless smile. "Nah, I just have bad luck. Do you want to hear the story of why it's not my fault, Scarecrow?"

"No," he said.

He led the way across the parking lot to his car. Naturally, it was a sleek modern affair, just tiptoeing up to the line of being ostentatious. Spotlessly black, it was probably the cleanest car in the lot. I immediately wanted to coerce a flock of pigeons into a well-timed fly-over, but the sky was empty of my allies.

"So," I began, "Twenty-five years . . ."

"Twenty-three."

". . . and here you are doling out my bail." I popped open the passenger door and hopped into the car. The interior was as clean as the outside. A pair of expensive-looking sunglasses lay neatly in the center console. I picked them up and put them on, grinning at my reflection in the side mirror. "We're not brothers, but we're not enemies today either, eh?"

Kakashi slid in next to me, his cold aura filling the car, turning the cozy leather interior suddenly claustrophobic.

"Not enemies today, *tengu*, no," he said. He wrapped his unnaturally long fingers around the wheel, seeming to hesitate. "As a matter of fact, it seems I may require your help."

I laughed out loud, a startled squawk. Having grown accustomed to wearing my touch of telepathy like a pair of old boots, I'd forgotten how much fun it was to be surprised.

"Say that again!" I pleaded, still cackling. "Kakashi the immovable, Kakashi of the shining sickle, asking for help from old Johnny Crow! I oughta make you beg! No, I want a boon. A big one! Carte blanche, brother! I want . . ."

He reached out quicker than I could track, his fingers suddenly cold against the skin of my throat. My laughter died so fast it was like he'd turned it off by touch alone. My very long life took a quick sprint before my eyes, but he only rested his fingers lightly against my pulse, studying me.

"This is new," he commented.

It took my mind a moment to claw its way past instinctive panic, but I eventually remembered the trio of raggedy black feathers that I'd had Bug Torres ink onto my neck during my last stint inside.

"Well, that's another nice perk of the big house," I croaked. "Good stories and cheap ink."

All the bluster was gone from my voice. Even after Kakashi sat back, I could still feel the ghost impression that his touch had left on my skin. Bastard had a way of making me feel pretty damn mortal.

He waited, silent. I stalled, petulant. Muttered a curse in the old language. English wasn't expressive enough to sum up my feelings sometimes.

"What kind of help?" I grumbled.

If the old boy actually had the facial mobility to smile, I think he would have but he only nodded in satisfaction and started the engine.

"I have been hunting one of my kind in these last weeks," he told me. "We believe he has gone mad. Become dangerous."

I snorted quietly. A dangerous scarecrow? The mind fairly boggled.

"I have been tasked with his elimination," he continued, ignoring me.

"Can't help you with that," I said. "Killing scarecrows? Too damn rich for my blood."

"I've been unable to even locate him. He has proven elusive."

"Well, of course he has," I sighed.

He glanced over at me, though he also could have been checking behind us as he backed out. "Explain."

I shrugged and pushed the borrowed sunglasses up on my nose, relaxing against the sun-heated leather of the upholstery. I pretended that I was a pat of butter melting onto fresh baked bread.

"You're the same as him," I said. "Same powers, same tricks . . . It'd be like me trying to take down Magpie. We'd chase each other in circles until rain started falling up."

We pulled out onto the highway and Kakashi nudged the car up to speed, the engine purring like a contented mountain cat.

"You believe I would be wise to seek the advice of someone whose mind runs counter to mine," he said quietly. "Someone whose natural instincts go against everything that my people believe."

I nodded. "Them's the breaks, brother. Every so often, you proud boys need to hop down into the muck with the rest of us and . . ."

He glanced at me and his hell-black eyes were twinkling. I realized the tidy little corner that I'd talked myself right into. Perfect. Now the stubborn bastard thought I agreed that he needed me.

"Any of us could do it for you," I said. My attempted nonchalance fell flat. "I mean, I'm not the only bird still spitting prophesy on the western seaboard, old man. And most of 'em have less history than you and I."

Kakashi and Crow, trying to work together. Hysterical. It wasn't going to be a buddy-cop movie; it was going to end in blood and panic and fury and maybe a death that stuck this time.

He shook his head. "We balance each other, *tengu*. Yin and yang, dark and light. Stronger together."

I peered at him, head cocked to the side. "You didn't feel that way in '44."

I'd had to regrow both my hands. Took the better part of the year. Sometimes still hurt in cold weather.

"I was younger then," he said, immovable. "And you were more foolish."

I thought I'd been doing those people a pretty big kindness, showing them a sneaky way out of the internment camp. But I'd always been better at 'spur of the moment' rather than big plans and the guards had started shooting and then people were screaming and running. Someone kicked over a stove and then one of the main buildings went up like dry tinder and Kakashi had come striding through the woodsmoke, his sickle gleaming red with reflected fire. To clean up my chaos and to teach me a valuable lesson.

I really hated Kakashi's valuable lessons.

I found myself massaging the bones of my wrist, thinking it over. If I did this, he would owe me. It wasn't in my nature to turn up my nose when something that good fell into my lap.

"You still don't eat, do you?" I asked.

"I do not. You do not need to either."

"But I *like* to eat. Tell you what," I said, "Stop calling me *tengu* 'cause I'm not one of your peoples' damn 'heavenly dogs,' and stop for fries on the way to wherever you're taking me, and you've got yourself a deal. I'll work with you, to do this."

Kakashi shot me another one of those looks, the closest thing to a smile that he could muster.

I didn't need prophesies to tell me this was going to end ugly.

Kakashi's little downtown apartment was like his car: modern, clean, elegant, and more than I could afford. I hadn't expected anything different. While he hung up his jacket, I took a stroll around the place, poking through the bookcase and snooping fruitlessly through the barren kitchen cupboards. I gave the fireplace a wide berth; he'd mounted his weapons above the mantelpiece, the simple wooden club crossed with that damn sickle like a coat of arms. It made my bones ache to look at them.

"Please, make yourself at home," Kakashi said, his tone even drier than usual.

I grinned at him and went to play with his expensive-looking stereo system, gleefully rearranging all the carefully balanced dials until the bass throbbed like a distant drum and the strident guitars had been all but obliterated.

"Of course, brother," I said. "Shut the curtains for me, would you? Visions are easier to see in the dark."

He did as I asked, which was a novelty that I didn't have nearly enough time to savor. The room was still too sterile, a bleached modern carapace. Inducing a vision here would be like trying to work a card trick without hands. Which, believe me, was harder than it looked.

Hunting down the thermostat, I cranked the heat as high as it would go then hunkered down to unlace my boots and chucked them aside with my socks. Kakashi watched me, a motionless silhouette in the gray light that seeped in through the curtain.

"What do you need?" he asked.

I sighed, curling my bare toes into the carpet as I stood up to strip off my jacket and shirt. "Smoke and drums and sweat and fire. I miss the old ways, my brother. Do you ever catch yourself thinking that you just want to go home, and then remember this is the same world you've always lived in?"

My old counterpart watched me in silence for a long moment, then moved over to the fireplace and flipped a switch. Weak colorless electric flames sprung up around a sculpted log tucked safely behind a layer of glass. I snorted, then snickered, and then I was laughing so hard that I had to brace my hands on my knees.

"That's *terrible!*" I exclaimed. "The worst excuse for fire I've ever seen! Oh, this delicate century . . ."

"I don't like fire," Kakashi said primly. "Pull yourself together, Crow. I do have a drum."

He slipped into the next room while I collected myself. I shut my eyes and swayed there in the quickly warming darkness, trying to feel the pulse of the earth beneath us. I shifted my weight from foot to foot, turning in a slow circle, taking deep breaths. Kakashi's return to the room was a low buzz of dissonance against my senses.

"What do you need?" he asked again, quietly.

"Drum for me," I said. Bobbing my head, I turned through my circle again, stomping my foot against the carpeted floor to show him the beat.

He took up the rhythm, too stiff and careful at first, but gradually improving until it amplified the rhythm of the earth and caught time with my heartbeat. Bending towards the ground, I hummed low in my throat, keeping my eyes shut, and I danced. I danced out a prayer and a plea, and I danced for an answer.

Where is he? Where is this rogue scarecrow?

Falling deeper into the dance, I let my drifting mind sneak past the sharp-edged disruption of Kakashi and slip into the streams of fate where prophesies spawned and a hundred possible futures glistened with untold potential.

I want to see him.

I felt my mind caught and irresistibly pulled through time, skipping into the near future. My final plea slipped from me half-formed and hardly considered.

Show me the place where Kakashi will be able to kill him.

Meat and feathers, the stink of fresh blood and salt water. A strong hand plunged down into an open torso and I heard the crackle of already broken ribs being shoved aside. Twisted burlap fingers stained dark red were wrenched out of the chest, trailing gore. The creature crammed the fistful of dripping meat into his gaping mouth. Wooden teeth crunched and squelched, black eyes gazing dispassionately down at the meal pinned in a crumpled heap under his filthy knees.

And I knew the guy. Son of a bitch, I *knew* that sorry mess of meat lying on the ground, eyes fixed and staring, blood dripping from spiked indigo hair. Blue Jay. Too late for the poor bastard now, caught halfway between forms and no longer whole enough to be patched back together, a puzzle of torn flesh and broken feathers. His ripped chest steamed slightly in the cool ocean air.

Two things occurred to me at once like a one-two punch taking my breath away. One: Kakashi knew about this guy. Knew he was a bird-eater out of control, knew how dangerous he was, and that he was wandering around my home turf. What the hell was he playing at? I would have been safer behind bars with this rogue on the loose.

The second thing, which eclipsed the importance of the first in a heartbeat, was that the rogue had stopped eating and was looking at me. *Looking* at me as my mind hung invisible within the vision.

If I'd had a body at the time, I think I would have pissed myself.

Hey there, good-looking, I thought weakly, and tried to skedaddle out of the trance.

Unlike Kakashi, this scarecrow no longer bothered with the veneer of humanity. When he opened his mouth, strings of burlap hung in blood-sodden strands over that dark opening, and I could see the rotting clumps of straw poking through the tears in his plaid shirt. Ants crawled like his madness under the worn material and a few spilled from his raggedy cuff as he stretched out his arm towards me as though he meant to grab me. As though he *could* grab me. That wasn't right; scarecrows had their fear and birds could dance through visions and never the twain should meet.

What exactly had he been eating along with the meat of us?

With a horrifying lurch and a bone-jarred shock of pain, I felt myself suddenly drawn towards him. My mind began to tear free from the anchor of my body and panic exploded within me. I clawed backwards, upwards, anything to get away from that widening mouth, but everybody knows it's impossible to run away from monsters in a dream and I was slipping.

With one last desperate struggle, I surged back towards my body and felt some other power catch hold of me there. I had become the rope in a vicious tug-of-war between two strong, cold powers and it hurt, it hurt in impossible ways that I hadn't known I could hurt. Every part of me that had the capacity to scream did. The vision began to collapse as I fought to get out of there, the edges of reality blurring and possible futures swirling around me like images in a kaleidoscope.

Through the pain and panic, I saw the vision continue to play out, fast-forwarding in confusing stops and stutters. I smelled blood and rot, and saw myself creep up behind Kakashi and set the back of his suit jacket on fire. Saw him go up just like the tinder he was made of. The vision churned wildly. I saw the rogue scarecrow dropping in smoldering clumps while Kakashi clawed at his own burning clothing, his hair. I saw myself explode into my treasured flock form, my mind fragmenting into thirteen parts as my dozens of wings beat at the fire hot air, and together we dove, all the parts of myself driving towards Kakashi as he staggered backwards with real fear in those eyes that had always been so blank . . .

I snapped back to my body in a defensive huddle on Kakashi's living room floor. My throat was raw like I was still breathing in the fiery air, but I thought maybe I'd just been hollering. Kakashi had a death grip on my shoulders and there were little black feathers gleaming around me on the floor in the weak antiseptic light from the fireplace. I picked one up unsteadily and examined it, giving a croaky laugh before blowing it out from between my fingers.

"Open the blinds," I rasped. "It's done."

Kakashi seemed hesitant to let go of me, but got to his feet and walked over to let the sun back in.

"You know where he is?" he asked.

I sorted through the jumbled vision, putting helpful details into one mental pile and all the disturbing shit into another heap. Like the fact that I'd seen a future where two bird-scarers had been killed with one stone. Where I'd seized up another shiny opportunity that had fallen into my lap, bright with spreading fire, and looked out for number one just like I always had. But right now was the time to focus.

I remembered the bridge with vivid detail and the distinct, red graffiti painted on its underbelly. I'd camped out there a time or two, snatching treasures from the cargo ships as they cruised into the harbor, enjoying the ocean air and harrying the sailors.

I nodded. "Yeah. Yeah, I know where to find him. Blue Jay's a dead man. I don't think we'll be in time to stop that."

Kakashi was already moving to the fireplace, switching off the flames and reaching to remove his sickle from the wall. "Then let us go before any others must die."

Others like me? Or like him? Like the humans packed into this city, as fragile as kittens? What exactly was on the potential chopping block when something as strong as a scarecrow lost their mind? And where did Kakashi's priority lie?

I thought it but didn't ask aloud, watching as Kakashi swung the polished sickle in a graceful arc. It cut through the air with a faint whoosh. Scary bastard. Glad he was on my side at the moment. For the moment.

I gathered up my shirt and boots, moving for the door. "Let's go," I agreed.

Kakashi was all but silent on the drive, despite my attempts to plant the seeds of conversation, and that left me a little too much time to think. Every red light and traffic jam detour had me grinding my teeth. I'd really liked Jay and nobody deserved to go out like that. Not for the first time, I decided the world had been much more fun before the scarecrows came about.

At long last, the bridge rose up before us, resplendent with the setting sun shining through it.

"If he destroys me," Kakashi said, "I leave it to you to spread the word to the others. Warn them. Do what you must to get away."

"Aren't you sweet," I muttered, popping open his glovebox and rummaging through it to distract myself. "I already know how this goes down. He dies, brother. Trust me on that much."

He nodded, satisfied. "Put my pressure gauge back, Crow. You don't even need that."

I sighed and put it back where I'd found it, but palmed a shiny little Zippo to make up for the loss. "This isn't your first rodeo, is it?" I commented. "You've done this before."

Kakashi hesitated, but nodded once.

I propped my boot against the dashboard, enjoying his resulting wince. "This didn't used to be part of your job description," I said.

"No," he said softly. "It was not necessary."

I whistled low, rubbing my hands over the knees of my jeans. "So it's true. The scarecrows are slipping their gears. Losing the plot. Out to lunch. Got a few bats in . . ."

"We are endless creatures with a purpose that has ended," Kakashi broke in. His voice was so damn sad that it shut me up. "Those we serve no longer need us. Modern technology offers more elegant solutions than we could hope to provide."

It was true enough. I couldn't remember the last time I'd seen a scarecrow standing guard in a farmer's field. Now it was all motion sensors and noise machines and static bursts. Scarecrows had become the quaint novelty of farmers' markets and Thanksgiving kitsch. My people had mostly forgotten me, but at least I hadn't been *replaced*.

"I'm sorry," I said, and I meant it. I probably should have stopped there, but the words tumbled off my tongue before I could stop them. "So when are you going to crack? Because I really think you ought to do me the favor of a two week running start, after all we've been through."

He made a noise, kind of like a laugh with most of the joy bleached out of it. "Not for a very long time, I imagine. My people still have some small need of me. I protect them when I am able." He looked at me and I think I was getting better at seeing the glimpses of humor in his dark eyes. "Besides which, you've proven yourself somewhat of a full-time occupation since we met. Your sense of fun, my reckless friend, may provide enough work for me to last through eternity."

I snickered and shook my head. "Well, I'm mighty flattered, wooden-man. Or maybe that's just hysteria setting in." But as the car slowed, reaching our destination, I found that I was smiling.

We parked the car just off one of the streets that funneled onto the bridge and started out on foot from there. Kakashi had turned tense and silent, his sickle tucked under his jacket. The gravel crunched under our boots as we went off the path and started down the slope to get beneath the bridge.

"I can feel him," Kakashi murmured. "He is here."

"Told you, didn't I?" I said. I could feel the presence of the rogue buzzing against my nerves too, like the whine of power lines in high wind. "Are you scared?"

The shadow of the bridge fell over us and it felt suddenly colder.

"No, Johnny," Kakashi said, "I am not. Are you?"

I shook my head, stuffing my hands into the pockets of my jacket, turning the stolen lighter over and over in my nervous fingers. "Nah."

We trudged a little further. The hairs on the back of my neck were standing on end and goosebumps rushed down my arms. Kakashi slid the sickle out from under his jacket.

"Were you lying a little just now?" I asked.

"Perhaps," he said.

I grinned. "Perhaps me too."

The rogue was where I had seen him in the vision, tucked up against the thick concrete struts of the bridge, hunkered down over poor Jay's mangled body, red to the elbows. When he looked up this time, it was Kakashi that his eyes went to, not me. He rose to his feet, an unnatural unfolding, and held out his arms to Kakashi, his bloody mouth twisting into a monstrous smile. He greeted him like a friend. A friend who'd brought a snack to share. Sudden fear gripped my bones, pooled in my kneecaps, and left my legs shaking.

At my side, Kakashi bellowed out some sort of kung fu battle yell and dropped into a ready stance, and I could feel the icy waves of induced fear flowing out from him so thick that I imagined for a moment I could see them. The rogue snarled in betrayal, his wet fingers clenching into fists, and I sure as hell felt the moment when his terror crashed into Kakashi's. The air wavered and warbled as it would above a fire, and I was shaking so hard my bones felt like they were going to pieces.

Kakashi growled low in his throat and the rogue staggered back a step. The pressure of their grappling powers intensified, like thunderstorms colliding. My ears popped and my eyes watered fiercely. I locked my chattering teeth onto my tongue to keep myself from throwing up, but my knees were betraying me and I was sinking, falling . . .

Kakashi's glance flicked over to me and the pressure dissipated as suddenly as an electric fireplace being switched off. The rogue's final blast of fear broke over us like a wave and I could felt the strange dark wrongness of it, could almost taste it. It made Kakashi's aura of fear feel like clean mountain air in comparison and I shuddered uncontrollably.

"Better go put him down, killer," I muttered to Kakashi. "Scream real loud if you need me."

Kakashi nodded once and darted in front of me. The rogue trampled over Jay's body and charged down the slope towards us, kicking up loose stones, his wet mouth opening wide in a raspy roar. Kakashi swung his blade, but the force of the rogue's charge took them both down in a messy tangle. I sidestepped, skittering back. I'd only seen Kakashi fight with all his strength a few times before, and each time reminded me that I never wanted to see it again. But the rogue was fast and violent, clawing at Kakashi's face, painting them both with Jay's blood. He was in too close for Kakashi to take another swing, so they grappled with each other, rolling over and over. I heard Kakashi's jacket tear on the rocky slope. It was taking all my will not to follow my instincts and get *out* of there. This was not a place for Johnny Crow.

I forced myself to take a step towards the pair, just as the rogue darted in like a snake and bit Kakashi's shoulder with an audible crunch. Kakashi grunted in pain and took a wild, clumsy swing with the sickle, tearing the rogue's side. Straw and rot spilled onto the rocks and the rogue untangled himself with a nerve-jangling wail, making a break out from under the shadow of the bridge.

"Quickly, after him!" Kakashi stumbled to his feet, his hand clasped against his shoulder but his face still unnervingly expressionless despite the clear pain in his voice. He sprinted up the slope and I followed, hopping over clumps of bug-infested straw.

Out from under the shadow of the bridge, I was blinded for a moment by the setting sun and had to blink away sunspots. Squinting, I realized the rogue had broken a rule that Kakashi and I had almost always managed to maintain; he'd taken the fight out in front of the humans. He was running up the walking lane at the side of the bridge, ricocheting drunkenly off the guardrail, and Kakashi was on his heels. Cursing under my breath, I gave chase.

Putting on a burst of speed, Kakashi swung again and took one of the rogue's legs out from under him. I nearly crashed into them both as the chase came to a messy halt.

"Stay away from him, Johnny!" Kakashi cried and swung for the rogue's neck, but the other scarecrow threw his arm up to block the blow. The blade hissed through cloth and rotten straw and something thicker that tore another howl from the rogue. The rogue had Kakashi in a death grip with his remaining hand before the severed arm had even hit the ground. Kakashi was at a bad angle and couldn't get a shot in, and the rogue was pulling him down, his bloody teeth chomping viciously as he tried to take another bite out of him while they grappled.

I danced around behind Kakashi in a helpless frenzy, unarmed and sorely outmatched. I'd get torn to shreds in my feathered form, even flying as the flock, and all that I had on me was a stupid lighter that'd be no good to anyone since I couldn't get past Kakashi to safely set the rogue on fire. It would be so easy! The bastard was made out of dry straw.

A thought struck me with such force that, for a moment, I went hot and cold all at once. I couldn't reach the rogue to burn him. But I could sure as hell set them both on fire from here.

As with most of the major choices I'd made in my life, I acted before I could think about it too hard.

It took maybe three seconds. The lighter was in my hand, a snap and spark, a quick lunge in, and Kakashi's back erupted in a sheet of flame. He cried out, his sickle clattering to the ground, and I backed away from him, my heart thumping. He groped at his back like he could grab the spreading flame and cast it away from himself, but he only succeeded in catching his arms on fire. Mindlessly, the rogue snarled and lurched in to sink his teeth into Kakashi's cheek just as the fire billowed up to engulf them both.

I'd fantasized about setting Kakashi on fire dozens of times. Maybe even hundreds, while I was waiting for my hands to regrow. It had given me a bitter kind of pleasure. But now that I'd done the deed, the only thing I felt was horrified regret at destroying one of my last constants in this new world.

The rogue's scream tore through me with a final blast of terror, but it was all over for him. He dropped away from Kakashi in clumps that fell with heavy thuds and spatters, stinking black smoke pouring up from them. Ants and earwigs fled the burning heaps in a steady stream.

And still, Kakashi burned, staggering like he was drunk. Wood burns slower than straw. He burned slower . . .

I burst into my feathered form, felt myself scatter into the flock as I plunged through the smoke towards my old nemesis, my sometimes friend. I battered at him with my wings, driving him back, shoving and carrying and clawing until I pushed him over the guardrail and sent him tumbling like a comet towards the river below. My wings were singed, a whole lot of feathers burnt to the nubs, but I swooped down after him. He met the water with a hard splash and when he sank, he wasn't moving.

I hit the river as the flock, thirteen individual splashes, and then reformed myself under the freezing water. The shock of salt water against my burns left me choking as I broke the surface, but I took a gulp of air and dove under again, swimming for the bottom.

Let me tell you, waterlogged wood is *not* fun to drag through a fast-moving current. It wasn't pretty, but I managed it, keeping my fist locked in the collar of his jacket as I kicked and paddled for the shoreline. By the time I got there, I barely had enough strength to haul Kakashi out of the water and I'd swallowed half an ocean in the process. I dropped to my knees beside him and turned him over.

The old boy was in rough shape. His outer shell was mostly burned away, the veneer of flesh clinging in ragged patches, the bare wood beneath black. But he was looking at me and making feeble little movements. Still alive. I was so relieved I could have kissed him.

Water dribbled from the sides of his ruined mouth with a garbled sound. He made a blind grab for me and managed to find my boot with his charred hand. The words were a mess when he forced them out, but I understood them. "Thank . . . you . . . Crow . . ."

I cackled and flopped down on my back next to him, letting the last of the setting sun dry us out. The cars on the bridge rumbled past above us, the humans untouched by what had just brushed up against the edges of their lives.

Destiny's a funny bird. I hadn't really thought about it at the time, but the vision had played out just as I'd seen. The only thing that I'd misunderstood was the motivation.

The world was changing, faster and faster, but Kakashi would always be Kakashi. Scarecrows didn't make much sense without Crow and, to speak the truth, there'd be a hole in my world without the old devil around too. Maybe he wasn't as crazy as I thought when he said we were stronger together. Maybe, as usual, he was just able to see a bit further than I could.

I glanced over at him again, studying him. He looked back up at me, pain mixed with patience. Yes, I was getting better at reading him. Maybe his current lack of skin helped a little.

"We're going to have to do something about your face," I said. "It's uglier than usual."

I sat up, shaking the river out of my hair, and offered my hand to him.

"Lucky for you," I told him with a grin, "I happen to know a guy. And he owes me one."

My old heart beat in my chest once. Then twice. Then Kakashi reached up and grasped hold of my hand.

THE ROOFNIGHT

Amanda C. Davis

When Quentin Meeks set out from the base of Mount Whiterock, he had a donkey, his best surveying equipment, a kit of high-quality travel gear, and two commissioned jobs from Duke Greeble—one explicit, and one secret. By the time he poked his head over the summit, his kit was down to the barest necessities (still, of course, high-quality) and he was starting to think neither commissioned job was worth the trouble.

His donkey remained some distance below him, feeding vultures. Quentin had tucked the surveying equipment nearby. He expected to collect it on the way back down. After all, you didn't strictly need to survey a town to gather its census—the surveying was a bit of extra fun. (Quentin, despite his adventurous occupation, had an academic's idea of fun.) And investigating the town for the presence of a smuggling ring of high-potency foreign liquor known as "glint"—why, that hardly needed any equipment at all.

He had no sooner crawled onto a packed flat of dirt that might well be the start of a path, than he spotted his first resident of Mount Whiterock.

She was about six years old. She was walking a rag doll along a fallen log and pretending that the dolly was tumbling to its death. Inauspicious. But after two weeks with no companion save a live donkey and, later, a dead donkey, he was willing to talk to anyone.

"Hello," said Quentin.

She gave him a steely, appraising look. Her rag doll took another deadly plunge. "Who are you?"

"I'm Mister Meeks. I'm from the government."

"The what?" said the girl.

He had expected this. He hoisted his teetering knapsack, and tried to look like anything but the muddy, stooped, skewed-spectacled man he was. "Why don't you take me to your mother? I'm sure she's heard of us."

The girl looked doubtful, the rag doll doubly so. But she stood up and gave Quentin an impatient "come with me" gesture. He followed eagerly.

Soon the great jagged stones of Mount Whiterock parted to show a village sprouting from the dry soil. Quentin heaved his burden along behind his guide, openly marveling. Every plot had a garden and a cottage pieced together from the garden's first bounty: rocks. In most of the gardens stood a pole that impaled two baskets, in the stylistic shape of a person.

"What a lovely village," said Quentin.

"You smell like dogs," said the girl.

She led him to a house where a woman sat on the stoop, weaving another garden-pole basket. The woman did him the favor of pretending not to see them until they were within speaking distance. When they were, she squinted up at them and said, "Janiza! Leave that poor man alone."

"Oh no," said Quentin, "she's been very helpful. Quentin Meeks," he added. "I'm here to take a census of Mount Whiterock."

The woman's hands slowed in her basket-weaving, which still left them at a pretty impressive pace. She was a red-faced, broad-shouldered type. "A census."

"It's a commission to count the citizenry. From Duke Greeble."

"I've heard the term," the woman snapped. "Greeble. Is that who's Duke now?" She grabbed her mostly-finished basket and stood. "Janiza, run and get your brothers and sisters for dinner." The little girl darted off. "You look like you've got a heavy burden there, Mister Meeks."

31

"It's loathsome," said Quentin, who hated to dissemble. "I'm sorry, I didn't catch your name."

"Martle Eadly."

"Martle, I hope you can tell me where I might be able to stay for the night. I'll pay, of course."

She looked him over. Her gaze was unnervingly thorough. "It's nearly nightfall. You best stay in my house. Go on in. The sick room's empty, and it's clean, too. Give you somewhere to throw down all that kit. You should have brought a donkey."

"My donkey died," said Quentin.

The woman's laughter was ungracious but at least, Quentin thought, it was genuine.

Inside, a couple of young people of a familiar red-faced, broad-shouldered type showed him to the sick room, where he unloaded his gear and took a moment to stand there being grateful the weight was gone. The inside walls were plastered to hold in the heat from the kitchen fire and for a stone hut on a desolate hill, it was surprisingly comfortable. Martle Eadly's hospitality was almost enough to make him feel sorry about investigating her, and her town, over some unlicensed glint.

Almost.

Janiza appeared in the doorway. "Mama said I should tell you to come eat." She dashed away without waiting for a reply.

Quentin emerged into the kitchen. The young people had multiplied. Several were bustling around with dinnerware and several more were already seated. In addition, there was a mild-faced, bearded man at the end of the table opposite the fireplace.

"Hello," said Quentin.

The man raised a noncommittal hand as if accustomed to strangers appearing around the table for dinner.

"My family," said Martle, from the fireplace. "Everyone, this is Mister Meeks. He's taking a census."

"Where is he taking it?" said an older boy.

"You en't that ignorant or that funny," said his mother. "Make a place for Mister Meeks."

The young people obliged. Of them, Janiza was clearly the youngest; he placed the oldest at fifteen or so. Martle began filling plates from a kettle over the fire, and the children passed them around in a surprisingly orderly way. Quentin accepted his plate gratefully.

"Sit," said Martle.

It was a quiet and unimpressive command, but it was obeyed with rigor. Quentin sat where he was put. He dug in.

The food was some kind of boiled grain, surprisingly salty with a good flavor of game, and the first hot meal Quentin had eaten in weeks. He relished the moment. The moment passed much quicker than he intended.

"That's an appetite," Martle observed. She nodded to the oldest boy, who got up and refilled the plate. "I hate to think what you've been eating lately."

"I hate to tell you," said Quentin. He filled his mouth again. "Mmmfmazing. I can't thank you enough."

"No need," said Martle. Still, there was a hint of the merchant in her voice that made Quentin wonder if she had something in mind. Surely she didn't suspect why he was here . . . ?

The bearded man, the presumed Mr. Eadly, said, "Agnis tells me to expect the Roofnight tomorrow."

"Is that so?" said Martle.

"So says Agnis."

"Ah, she would know."

Quentin perked up. "The Roofnight? Is that a local celebration? I adore local celebrations."

"More work than fun," said one of the oldest boys. By the looks of things, Janiza had the honor of kicking him under the table, though there were many contenders.

"It's both," said Mr. Eadly mildly. "Harvest of sorts. You came at a special time of year, Mister Meeks."

"How lucky," said Quentin. "I should love to participate, if you'll allow me."

"I don't see why not," said Mr. Eadly.

Mr. Eadly didn't, but Quentin did: nothing loosened a tongue like a local celebration. He let his eyes roam the house while the children described their respective days. The place was rustic and rugged, with nothing frivolous: even the decorative pots and pans that hung from the ceiling were still pots and pans. (He thought of the baskets on poles in every field. Perhaps these people kept their ornamentation out of doors.) No house would allow a shipment of glint to pass by without taking a share . . .

His eyes lit on a corked jug behind the firewood.

Quentin's eyebrows did a delighted dance. He knew without checking what was inside that jug—although he'd check, unquestionably, before making his report, and probably load some into his pack as proof. The suspicions of the capital would be confirmed. There was glint in this village. And where there was a little, there was almost always a lot.

Nobody in Duke Greeble's kingdom knew how the northern witches made their glint, although the intelligentsia (among which Quentin counted himself) believed it was magically extracted from flowers that only grew far outside of their borders. But it was getting to them somehow, and Mount Whiterock, so close to the northern border and so far from the Duke's authority, would be a smuggler's dream. Finding glint here explained so much about how it seeped through the kingdom. And finding that would go a long way toward stopping it. At least in untaxed form.

Quentin said, in a voice of innocent curiosity, "Now, that jug—"

"I expect you travel a lot," said Martle.

It was, Quentin, reflected later, exactly like throwing a stone into a flock of birds. Martle's children burst into questions and excited gestures and chatter about what they had heard about other places that they were *sure* were true but could Quentin please confirm? It's just they told their best friend something and they didn't believe them . . .

He answered what he could and laughed off the rest, but what he failed to do was keep an eye on the glint jug, because when he finally tried to get a good long look at it after dinner, it was no longer there.

〜

Quentin began his census at the crack of dawn, in the best way he knew how: with a map.

All his best surveying tools were halfway down the mountain with his donkey, so he paced it out. The main street wound directly from the mountain pass to the mouth of the mine. Along it were stone houses, clearly constructed of leftover mountain, four and five deep, peppered with gardens and surrounded by fields that Quentin guessed were half root vegetables, half stone. Quentin started at the mine and began marking down residences as he came to them.

The man at the first house said, "What are you doing?"

The woman at the second house said, "Get off my land." She leaned across her porch railing to the man at the first house. "Who is this? Have you ever seen him before?"

"I'm Quentin Meeks," Quentin told them both. "Duke Greeble has sent me to take your census."

"You tell that greedy blue-blood we want it back," said the woman. It did not sound like a joke.

Quentin said, "May I come in? I'll be doing the official count over the coming days, but I'd love to get an idea of the layout of a typical home here."

The man gave a shrug. "If you must."

"Right now?" Quentin pressed.

"I don't see the harm." Nearby, the woman raised her hand and let it fall, as if she couldn't do much about the intrusion, but didn't care too much either.

Perhaps neither of them had any contraband. But the glint was somewhere. His attention swiveled back to the mine. A large underground space would be perfect for hiding a smuggled cache of glint. "I don't suppose I could take a tour of the mine as well? Only I'm so curious—"

"No," said the man, simultaneously with the woman, who added, "Nobody lives in the mine, you fool."

"Of course," said Quentin, with a deprecating chuckle. "What a silly notion."

Notion confirmed, he thought.

In fact (he thought, as he mapped all sixty-one of the town's residences on an increasingly smudged and wrinkled page) there seemed to be no mining going on at the moment, which boosted his suspicions further. Perhaps Mount Whiterock did no, or little, actual mining at all. Perhaps this town lied about its ore production and sent every grain of it to the capital, so it could focus on its real source of income. The more people he spoke with, the more sure he became, and the more fiendishly clever they seemed.

When his map was done he headed back to the Eadly house.

Mr. Eadly was on the porch, with his various children scattered within earshot. Quentin came up to him, in what he believed was a companionable way.

"Doing good work?" said Mr. Eadly.

"Things are going very well," said Quentin, truthfully. He indicated the mine. "I can't help notice no one seems to be going into the mine."

"It's nearly the Roofnight," said Mr. Eadly. "A few days off."

"I see," said Quentin. He sat, stretching his shoulders. He expected he'd be sore from his mountain trek for years. Curse that frail-constituted donkey. "Tell me more about this Roofnight. What does it entail?"

Mr. Eadly looked him over. "Ah, well," he said slowly. "It's not one of your riotous holidays, you understand. No revels in the streets." He pointed to the neighbor's field, where two women were settling a hat and coat on the pole-basket. "We set up our scarecrows a few days ahead."

"How festive," said Quentin.

"Then we all go into the town lodge and pass the night drinking and telling stories. It's a real contest to tell the best story. You should compete, Mr. Meeks. Just don't think your far-off tales are an easy win over our local ones. We have some frightful legends in these hills."

"I'm sure of it."

"Then in the morning we eat all the food we've had cooking in the embers all night, and drink a bit more to clear our heads, and go take down our scarecrows, and it's a day of rest before we all head back to work."

"In the mine?" said Quentin.

Mr. Eadly gave him a strange look. "Yes, in the mine. Or in the home, or what have you."

"I'm delighted to have come here when I did," said Quentin. "My timing was perfect."

It all added up too perfectly, he thought gleefully. The scenario was clear in his head. An evening when the village turned their backs on the mine, so they could claim to know nothing of what went on there. A dark, empty night and a big, private storage space. He might even catch the smugglers at work—!

No, no, that was too much for one man. He would confirm the plot and let the army take care of the rest. Good luck to them making the miserable trek. He hoped they had stronger donkeys.

He gazed at the mouth of the mine. What a brilliant scheme. He had to admire these mountain folk for their acumen . . .

An old woman came hobbling out of the mine.

Quentin stood. So did several others, he noticed. Doors opened. Martle came onto the porch, wiping her hands.

"It's tonight," the old woman called, her worn croak cutting through the air. "The Roofnight is tonight!"

"I thought no one was working in the mine today," said Quentin.

"Now who told you a thing like that?" said Martle. (Mr. Eadly chuckled.) She oriented Quentin toward the town lodge. He felt a hat being stuck onto his head. "Go on ahead now. Follow the children, they'll already be gathering. Janiza, make sure Mister Meeks doesn't get lost." Janiza appeared and took hold of Quentin's sleeve, like she would a dog's scruff. "Tell everyone to give Mister Meeks a good warm welcome."

"I hope I don't get in the way," Quentin said, while Janiza was dragging him to the town lodge, but the moment they arrived it became clear that getting in the way was simply the nature of the event. There were fires to be lit and chairs to be placed, barrels to be hoisted from the basement, preliminary drinks to be passed around. (Quentin gave his a sniff. Did he detect a glintish hint? Perhaps, though it wasn't strong.) He did everything they asked of him—even if it involved undoing what someone else had asked him to do.

After a hurried hour or so, the last town resident came into the lodge, the doors were barred, and the Roofnight began.

Quentin Meeks, widely-traveled but with a scholar's tendencies, found this among the pleasantest revelries he had been privileged to attend. It was jolly without being boisterous, lively without being loud. (Was there an anxiety in the air that muted the joy? Quentin couldn't say.) When the story contest began, he told about his friend the giantess of Duvolle and her love affair with a traveling bard. He was eliminated early. And while a much better storyteller explained what lurked in the shadows under the tallest trees in the woods, Quentin Meeks slipped out the back, into the empty village.

He moved as quickly as he could in the dark. Surely he would be missed soon.

At the entrance to the mine he took a pickaxe from the rack, intending to break the lock, but the door was wedged open. He swapped the pickaxe for a lantern, lit it, and entered the mine.

The low ceiling stooped him further than the equipment he had hauled up the mountain on his back. He held the lantern far out before him. At every branching tunnel he peeked inside, expecting to find the cache of crates or bottles or kegs that would prove the dukedom's glint came through here.

His lantern light caught on a hint of metal. Quentin turned. He knew just enough about glint production to recognize a still.

"Making your own?" murmured Quentin. "I haven't seen a flower on this whole mountainside . . ."

A hand closed on Quentin's arm.

He jolted as if he'd been gripped by a ghost, and whirled around, where he found to his relief that he had not been. It was Martle Eadly, deep furrows in her brow. "What are you doing down here?" she hissed, her voice a whisper. "Who sent you here?"

Quentin contemplated pretending to be lost. It didn't seem like it would work so instead he drew himself up. "Duke Greeble sent me, madam. And I suspect you know why!"

"Keep your voice down, you fool!" She grabbed for his arm again. Quentin dodged. "I mean which fool of my neighbors sent you into the mine tonight . . . never mind, I'll find out later. Come on! There's still time to get you safely into the lodge."

"I know what's going on here!" said Quentin.

"Do you now?" said Martle, her whisper brittle. "Then you'll come with me before—"

A thick rustling and chorus of high screeching rose like a tide from deep within the cave.

"What?" said Quentin stupidly.

The rustle grew to a roar.

Martle tackled Quentin to the ground. In a flash, something suspiciously like her sweater fell over their heads. It was not a moment too soon. The fluttering turned to heavy, sharp slapping of wings just above, and the squeaks rose to shrieks as a thick storm of *something* burst from the depths of the mine and zoomed past.

"What?" shouted Quentin, over the racket. It was the only word he could produce that was not a curse.

"Bats," Martle shouted back.

The next word out of Quentin's mouth was, in fact, a curse.

The flock blew past like a winter storm. Quentin imagined pricks and pokes at his head through the sweater—or perhaps didn't imagine. The burst of sound went far longer than Quentin would have expected. It trickled away slowly. The shrieks of the bats continued to echo down the mine far after their wings stopped stirring the breeze.

Quentin threw the sweater from his head. He scrambled to the wall. It was all he trusted. "This is the Roofnight?" he gasped. "Bats? Why didn't anyone mention the bats?"

"*I* meant to have you too drunk to notice them," said Martle, brushing the dirt from her knees. "Everyone else, I suppose they were trying to get you killed." Her face took a serious turn. "Tell me who it was sent you here. That wasn't right."

"I came on my own," Quentin admitted.

"Ah."

There was a beat.

"What do you know about the glint?" said Martle gently.

"We know it's smuggled through here," said Quentin, taking as much strength as he could from the authority not here to actually protect him. "Although I see you're producing it. Tax-free, of course."

"Of course," said Martle.

"I'll have to report it."

"I assumed as much."

Another beat of silence, this one more uncomfortable.

"Where do you get them?" asked Quentin.

"Hmm?" Martle raised her head.

"The flowers, the northern flowers you brew it from. Such a bizarre liquor. It's such a well-guarded secret. Indulge me, if you will."

"Flowers," Martle echoed. She covered a bray of a laugh. "I'll show you." She drew him to the door of the mine. "Hush," she said. "Look." They peered into the open night.

The night was not so very open after all.

Quentin's first thought was that he had not noticed so many trees scattered around the village. Then his eyes and his brain caught up with one another, and he sank back with a chill. In every garden, the scarecrows were flocked with bats so thickly they looked like leaves.

"You see now why we gather inside?" she murmured. "Stay back before a hundred of them mistake you for our bait."

"Yes, but where's the—"

One of the scarecrows snapped in half. A swarm of bats, gnawing and clawing, followed it to the ground.

Quentin Meeks, who had traveled from one end of the dukedom and learned hard lessons about when to retreat, backed further into the darkness of the mine.

He and Martle watched from the shadows as one scarecrow after another fell under the flocks of bats. When the nearest flock left its field, with a devastated scarecrow behind it, she gestured to the grass. Quentin squinted. In the moonlight he could see the brittle grass and stone had been coated with an amber-colored sludge.

"Flowers," Martle sniffed.

The taste of the beer he'd drunk earlier rose in Quentin's throat. "Oh," he said. "I see. How unappetizing."

"You get used to it," said Martle. "The scarecrows draw them into our gardens for long enough to make sure they drop it where we can get it. They save it up most of the year."

"I wish I had never asked," said Quentin.

"I know. Glint is some ugly stuff, but its trade goes a long way to making this mountain livable. Ore doesn't sell for what it used to, and you can't eat it." She crossed her arms. "I suppose this will cost us more in taxes than it's worth."

Quentin Meeks, who knew something of numbers, knew that was true. He thought of the salty, filling gruel, the warm plastered walls, the cheerful young people. He thought of the village massed in the town lodge to keep from being torn apart by bats. He thought of Martle slipping into the night after him, knowing what was coming.

"And yet," said Quentin slowly, "you'd have no new tax and no trouble if you'd simply left me to die in here."

Martle tilted her head. "Don't I know it."

Quentin nodded, deciding. "One thing I've learned in my travels, Mrs. Eadly, is to follow the example of the locals. And yours was a generous act."

She smiled. It occurred to him that her generosity in saving his life was perhaps not uncalculated.

When Quentin Meeks set out to return to Duke Greeble, he had a loaned donkey (that he swore he would return the moment bought one for himself), a thorough and accurate census of the town, and a definitive report stating that no glint was being smuggled through the town. It was quite true, of course. Quentin prided himself on honesty.

He also had a handful of friends in Mount Whiterock and a reason to never imbibe glint again. But he didn't put that in any of his reports. Some things, like the saving of one's life, simply could not be calculated.

He did, however, request reimbursement for the donkey.

SKIN MAP
Kim Goldberg

There is no misery to compare with that which exists where technology has been a total success. —*Thomas Merton*

Her skin glows a buttery yellow in the candlelight. She has taken to shutting off the main breaker each night so that she can escape the searing hum of frequencies, the scorch of ambient electromagnetic fields upon her skin. She used to read at night by flashlight until even the current of the two batteries became too much for her battered hide and viscera to withstand. Tiny white burns began to appear on the thin skin between the fingers of her flashlight hand. So out came the candles.

She takes long baths in Epsom salts to discharge the static build-up in her body and to replenish the magnesium leeched away from her tissues and blood by wireless radiation. That damned smart meter! They snuck it on her last house while she was overseas. When she returned, she had slept for two months with her head one foot from the accursed contraption before she discovered it was there and what it was doing to her. By then it was too late. Her finely tuned musician's brain had been baked like a raisinbread pudding, and she was about as mobile as one too. Most days she did not get out of bed.

She is better now in her new place. At least she can get up, make a cup of tea, move around her house avoiding the wall with the smart meter. (They are everywhere in Vancouver—like cockroaches, only bigger and more lethal.)

Each day she roams the deep forests of Stanley Park, letting the tall firs and cedars shield her from the sizzle of WiFi and texting. Her fiery skin cools as she watches the canvasback ducks and widgeon glide across the dark waters of Lost Lagoon. Park staff have scattered straw that the mallards and coots use for nesting. The shoreline is strewn with downy feathers.

Her skin has become a map of the hidden world of frequencies, its misty peaks and troughs etched by pinpricks of electricity scurrying like deer mice beneath her smoldering hide.

She covers her tender flesh with long-sleeved shirts and long skirts. She walks the forest and the lagoon edge. She walks the sea wall so as to be scrubbed clean by the soft breath of the Pacific one ion at a time.

One night she sleeps on a bed of damp moss and dreams she is a planet wearing a skin map. She wakes to a raven's raucous laugh splitting the new day in two—the world she came from, and the world that awaits her deeper in the forest. She ponders the logistics of gift giving and self-preservation. Specifically: is there a way she can give humanity the map it so clearly needs but cannot yet read, while simultaneously ridding herself of the scourge of her infernal burning skin? She calculates the price of maintaining a single identity. (And that price turns out to be mortality.)

She looks up at the cedar boughs above and notices the immaculate tight weave of their tiny scale leaves. How like a living fabric, a skin of sorts . . . She looks down at her feet and sees a cast-off skin of a northwestern garter snake. How like an ancient parchment with its subtle code of scales. And the snake was not harmed by leaving its skin behind, its gift to the world. She takes one last look at the trees and the new day through eyes she will no longer need in her new form. It was all so beautiful. Once. Before the spark and crackle of frequencies.

She must work quickly or there will be no gift to leave behind. She can already feel the tight weave of tiny scale leaves starting to form subcutaneously, the gentle emergence of xylem and phloem supplanting her tortured vascular system . . .

~

'STRAW WOMAN' DISCOVERED IN STANLEY PARK

VANCOUVER—In a gruesome case that has Vancouver Police stumped, a group of Japanese foreign exchange students discovered a life-size 'straw woman' that was clad in human skin at the base of a tree beside Lost Lagoon in Stanley Park.

The students, who have been eliminated as persons of interest in the case and are now receiving counselling, were feeding the ducks at the time of their discovery.

The victim's skin, which was somehow preserved in whole form, had been stuffed with leaves, feathers and straw. DNA tests have not identified whose skin was used for this ghoulish creation. However police say the skin belonged to a female and appears to be covered with fine tracings that may be some form of symbolic code. Photographs of the skin have been sent to experts in both the Languages and Mathematics departments at University of British Columbia for analysis.

A FIST FULL OF STRAW

Kristina Wojtaszek

Sometimes I forget that my face can change and my feet can move, and I get slugged by an exhausted coworker for standing around with a sewn-on grin. I can never keep track of shifts in time and spells undone, and often confuse the night shift with my day job as a scarecrow. Nights I stock spices and turn apples on store shelves for flighty shoppers, while by day I stare out over a bedraggled garden and nod at fickle birds. The problem is the jobs are too much alike. Except when *she* comes in. Because there is nothing in the world like her.

The apples blush beneath his calloused fingers as he stoops over them, his broad shoulders like folded wings under the fluorescent dawn. I can't help but watch him sometimes, standing there turning swells of red and gold and green in the hollows of the display hiding bruises or scars, so customers only see perfection. I wonder if he feels as I do, that one day has stretched on into a year, the lack of sleep grinding me down to a rough, woody ache. I have stepped too near. He lifts his head and neither of us can help our smiles. I want to ask him. *Do you? Ache?* Of course I don't dare, but ask instead, "Don't you ever get a day off?"

~

She appears suddenly, like the moon from behind a cloud, and my grin stretches at the seams. I could stand this way forever, just taking her in, but being more human than I, she feels the need to speak.

She comes in late while her children are asleep so she can shop without the toddler yanking on her hair and the older boy knocking tomatoes onto the floor. I know this because I used to work days, until the witch decided I was more useful to her during sunlight hours. Since the old woman provides most of the store's organic produce, she had no problem convincing the manager to switch my shift.

I can't seem to stop smiling as I stare at the spill of her hair, the very color of sun-warmed earth. I shrug, "I like to work. Keeps me busy." And I ask if there's anything I can help her find. "Actually," she says, holding up her tattered little grocery list. I'm beside her in an instant, so close I can smell her faux leather jacket and the Pantene Pro-V radiating from her hair.

⌾

He stands so close I can feel the heat from his skin. He's nervous, my grocery list trembling in his hand. I wonder if he can even read my horrible hand writing, but at last he says he knows where the turmeric is. "I can almost smell that one from here," he says, "it has such a distinctive scent." I've only just begun trying my hand at Indian cooking, pining for something new in the monotonous routine of dinner-making, so turmeric is a whole new spice to me, but I nod as though I know what he means. He finds it all too quickly, and I have no more excuse to linger, so I thank him and wheel away with my imprisoned produce. I wonder when it was that his elvish eyes first locked with mine and if he's ever gotten into trouble for all the bananas and apples he's slipped to my little boys over the last few months. He looks different, lately; a bit unkempt, probably from all the late night hours. "It's good to see you," he calls after me. I glance back a last time, taking in his 5 o'clock shadow and disheveled hair the color of straw.

⌾

My eyes ache as I watch her go. I touch them and find dampness, which amazes me because behind the glamour my eyes are nothing more than two charred holes in sackcloth where the witch once plunged her cigarette. I have no right, I know this. Not only because of the ring on her finger that shines like a fallen star, but because of who, *what*, I am. What would she do with stiff arms and a sagging chest full of spiders? I have no illusions; the witch reminds me often that I'm nothing but a charmed doll. But for all that I am not, I can't deny what this woman has stirred in me.

I crack open the bottle of turmeric as I head out into the night and almost choke in the overpowering aroma. And then I have a sudden, odd thought. I have no memory of his scent. Standing so close, I should have caught a whiff of coffee or soap, a hint of deodorant, maybe a haze of stale cigarettes . . . something. But as I wheel through a leaf pile in the parking lot, it hits me; the dry, clean scent of leaves. Leaves and apples. He smelled of nothing but autumn.

I am weary by the time my shift ends, though these aching legs, these burning eyes, are not mine. As I lean back into my post, I long for true sleep. I am not allowed to dream, though I sense it, the whispers of forgetfulness and scraps of desire closing upon me as the sky pales, then brightens. In this new dawn I am aware of something other than the nodding heads of corn and small eyed potatoes silently swelling underground. I notice something bitter in the breeze, even as my senses begin to dull. It is a cruel thing to lose your abilities and not your mind. As I return to my true shape, the memory of her remains. With nothing but a birch branch for a spine and a chest full of hay, still I love her.

⌒

I haven't slept for days, what with my toddler worrying holes in the night and my husband's endless snoring. I tell myself tonight is no different, but of course it is. I search the dark for the shape of his smile. Perfect and slow, it makes me think of a wide, white row of cemetery stones. I picture us there, in a place where no one cares anymore about what should and shouldn't be. I could lay down and rest in this dream, but of course that's all this is; a dream. I turn to the man asleep beside me, and remind myself that I love him.

⌒

I tremble against my rough post as a shadow swallows the stars. The witch has come to have a word with me. She lands with a flutter, her talons perched upon my wilting shoulder, and dips her head, mercury eyes taking me in. She plucks once at my collar and cries, "Who gave you permission to love?" I have no way to answer, of course, but she cocks her head at the sound of thought.

How can you not?

She takes this badly, her beak a dagger flashing in and out of my throat. "You are mine, you overstuffed sack of rot! Forget this woman." But she knows that I cannot. I've been out too long, steeped in humanity. For this, I will be punished.

The next day the witch gives my notice to the store manager, who will never see me again. She haunts the store every evening, scrutinizing each woman who comes and goes while I dangle without a will in her backyard.

⌒

A month goes by and I don't see him. I wonder if he's quit. I try to be glad for him, hoping he's found a better job, a better life. But the brilliance of the stars is almost painful, now, and the nights have gone frigid too soon.

As I leave the store, disappointed by his absence, again, I see a little old woman pushing her grocery cart into the road. I guess she must live across the street and the store manager probably doesn't mind. Better a cart than a car with some senior citizens; still, I can't bear to watch her struggling with the curb. But when I go to help, she yanks the cart away with surprising strength, then stares at me long and hard under the flickering street light. Suddenly her whole demeanor changes and the next thing I know I'm burdened with her groceries as she holds the door for me.

I see her framed in the kitchen window. It shouldn't be possible, but there she is. Spying the steaming mug between her palms, I gain a new and terrible understanding of the nature of my punishment.

As the old woman rises to the cry of the kettle, wishing to refill my cup (though I've yet to take a single sip) my eyes wander out beyond the window. The moon has conquered a thick knot of clouds, and by its light I can just make out a funny-looking figure standing at attention in the back yard.

She tilts her head to mirror the angle of my own and it sickens me, the way her neck appears broken, just as mine must. The November rains have come and I am not the same, sharp figure I used to be. I am mortified, to say the least, but I doubt she'll recognize me now. Still, the way she stares. The witch hobbles back into the room and I scream a silent warning, waving my arm stubs in the wind.

The old lady perks right up when I ask about her garden. I've got a black thumb, myself, and I tell her so, and this makes her grin even wider. Suddenly she's slipping back into her sneakers and yanking at the sliding glass door. I leave the tea behind as she rattles on about various herbs and their "homeopathic remedies." A floodlight flickers on, startling me with its brilliance, and I feign interest in her flowers as we shuffle across the uneven stepping stones. But as she treads into the weeds, I stand stricken at the sight of the strangely life-like scarecrow. It is more than uncanny, his resemblance to . . . But even as I shiver, barely able to tear my eyes away, the little old woman calls for me to follow. She is waist high in her overgrown garden, waving me over.

She looks away, but as she brushes past, I feel her snatch a fistful of straw from my sleeve. I watch, stunned, as she stuffs the scraps of me against her own covered wrist.

I am speechless as the old woman holds a bundle of nightshade aloft, raving about its curative properties. Isn't that stuff deadly? I worry she's lost her mind and might poison herself with her own "remedies." I really don't think she should be living alone. Then again, who am I to judge, with a sleeve full of stolen straw scratching at my wrist? I'm not quite sure what made me do it. I try desperately not to blush as I ask the woman if she'd consider selling her scarecrow.

As her fingers reach to her wrist, I notice the delicate flesh has already been scratched raw, and I am strangely aware of a deep throb that quickens into a steady rhythm. Her pulse echoes through my coarse body, and even though I haven't shifted, I can see her dull shoes as well as the sky.

The old woman laughs off my inquiry, steering me again toward the dark tangle of herbs. She wants to know if I'm sleeping well. How about my appetite? Her voice lowers as she confides that the heavy circles under my eyes suggest I've got a dark secret. I take a few steps back, edging my way toward the street. I feel invaded, as though she's fully aware of my nicked conscience and all the parasites of routine that gnaw at me. I can tell she's fishing for things, the way her eyes keep hold of mine. "Your husband ignores you, doesn't he?" I stumble back, and trip over a miniature picket fence.

She peers up at me from where she sits, sprawled on the grass from her fall, and to my astonishment, gives me a quick, triumphant smile before bounding off down the street. The witch hisses as she sheds her skin in the shadows and flies at me in all her feathered furry, but I am too distracted to care. While I still sense the stars above me, trapped with the witch in this tiny garden, I am elsewhere as well, seeing a cracked sidewalk flash into view beneath street lights and the flicker of running feet. The witch is plucking off my buttons, swallowing them one by one as she shreds my chest until I weep out all my straw.

Meanwhile I'm being lifted up in a lamp-lit room, watching a slow, careful smile; the very smile I live for.

My mind is clear as acid, though I haven't slept for days. I open my fist full of straw, unable to keep from grinning. I have more of him now than I ever hoped.

I am only half conscious of my sackcloth head as it lilts and finally falls, the witch screaming in a non-existent ear. The wind lifts the tattered chaff, scattering me across the moonlit yard and the streets beyond. Though the witch has lost her hold, her judgment has prevailed; if I cannot serve her in full, I will serve no one. I let go of what's lost, turning my mind to the little that matters. The better part of me is bent against the breast of the woman I love as she slides beneath her covers and sobs herself to sleep.

I dream that I am weeping seeds, enough to plant an orchard. He collects every one, my sorrows slumbering in his palms as we lay together in the sun. He shifts from man to straw, the scents of turmeric, apples, and dry leaves mingling as he pulls me close. He's finally earned his day off, one day that stretches on into years as he takes my hand in his stiff glove and presses it to the empty pocket over his heart.

JUDGE & JURY

Laura VanArendonk Baugh

Publisher's note: While this story stands on its own, readers can find the preceding narrative, "Sanctuary" by Laura VanArendonk Baugh, in the *Corvidae* anthology.

The courtroom had the weary air of people who deal with mortal decisions on a daily basis, and the earthy tones lingering from the seventies' decor did not improve the atmosphere

Still, the defendant looked more irritated than worried. He was lean, too thin for the suit he'd obviously borrowed. His hair was combed, probably at the advice of counsel, yet somehow still untidy and as the room filled, the jury settling restlessly into their seats, he looked around his lawyer toward the prosecutor's table. "Who do they have today?"

"Quiet," warned his lawyer. "Don't stare."

The defendant slouched back in his chair, his jaw set sulkily. He did not notice the man standing beside him. Nor did anyone else.

Junsuke Hirata, Ph.D. watched the defendant, and it was a curious and horrific sensation. He could not look away, could not move, could not speak even if anyone could have heard him. His chest was tight and his lungs constricted, and a distant part of his mind realized he was having a panic attack. Another fragment of rationality told him that was impossible, that he had no pulse to pound in his temples and no breath to catch. He was experiencing only what his subconscious thought he should, patterned by a lifetime of . . . *life*, when faced with a salient stimulus from a highly traumatic experience.

He swallowed against the pressure in his throat and drew a deep breath of what he knew wasn't air. He closed his eyes and exhaled, counting to twenty. Then he opened his eyes again and faced his murderer.

Everett Stapleton rested his joined hands in his lap, his lower lip protruding just slightly more than it should. This didn't surprise Jun; his every interaction with Everett had led him to conclude the young man was spoiled, entitled, and narcissistic, and being shushed at his own trial—where he should have been the center of all attention—had to chafe.

"All rise."

Everyone stood and faced the bailiff.

"The Superior Court of Bowman County is now is session, the Honorable Judge Maple Fieldhouse presiding. Please be seated and come to order."

Judge Fieldhouse was a handsome black woman with flecks of gray in her natural hair. Jun tried to remember if he had voted for her.

It was the trial's third day, and it was not a celebrity case, so the chairs reserved for public viewing were mostly empty. One reporter slouched in a rear seat, tapping at his phone, probably doing something other than note-taking.

"The People call Dr. Hollie Madison."

Jun walked to the prosecutor's table and took an empty chair, watching Dr. Madison approach the stand.

He had always liked Hollie. He hadn't realized exactly how much until after his death, when he had to face that he would never speak to her again. It was difficult for him to go more than a few miles from the station, he'd learned, and so he saw little of her these days. She had left the university after his death.

She kept her eyes well away from Everett Stapleton as the prosecutor questioned her. "And then did he say why he would stay the night at the lab?"

"Objection, hearsay," protested the defense attorney in rote.

"To the contrary, Judge, this is direct testimony and very relevant. The victim believed there was danger from the accused."

"It doesn't matter what he said to me," said Hollie, "it's all in a requisition letter. Jun asked for more security."

He had, though he hadn't thought anyone's life was in danger. He believed the activists would vandalize the building and equipment, perhaps try to frighten away the birds. He'd stayed the night, believing that when they saw the building was occupied, they would give up and leave.

He ignored the dance of legal protocol induced by the objection and Hollie's response, looking instead at the notes on the prosecutor's table. They included his letter asking for security cameras—deemed unnecessary for a lab which held a collection of children's toys and improvised puzzles, nothing considered valuable or tempting. The ornithology cognition research lab, to be fair, was a glorified pole barn.

The judge had given some directions to the jury to ignore the objection and following discussion, and now the prosecutor was speaking to Hollie again. "Dr. Madison, please describe for us the morning of March seventeenth."

Jun looked again to Hollie, and it felt as if his heart, which could not *be* beating, stopped. He had not been . . . *aware* during the discovery of his body.

Hollie nodded once, her face unnaturally still. She had schooled herself for this. "I called Dr. Hirata about eight that morning, to ask how the night had gone and whether any of the activists had shown up."

"Objection, the witness is implying my client was present without any actual knowledge."

"Your honor, the witness is only reporting her own intention."

"Objection overruled, please continue."

The interruption had rattled Hollie, and she was breathing more quickly now. Jun squeezed his fists.

"There was no answer, and so I thought I'd drive by. I didn't think—that is, I didn't really think anything had happened to him, just that maybe he'd forgotten to charge his phone or left it somewhere. So I drove out."

"Did you take State Road 800?"

"It's the only way out there. It took me about twenty minutes, but I could see the smoke when I was still a few miles out."

"And did you call police at that time?"

"Not yet. I was still—I was still hoping that nothing was really wrong, and I knew I'd see for myself in a few minutes. I didn't want to call for nothing, in case it was just trash or something." She licked her lips. "It was probably stupid, especially since we'd been worried about the activists. But hoping—sometimes denial seems like the most logical thing."

"What did you see when you arrived?"

"The building was partially burned, still smoking. There was debris everywhere. And—"

Her voice stopped, and she swallowed. Jun's stomach wrenched and he wanted to vomit. He wondered distantly if he even could.

"And by the driveway, where Kuebiko was—that is, we had a mascot scarecrow, and Dr. Hirata called him Kuebiko after a Shinto scarecrow spirit. But Kuebiko was gone, and . . . and Dr. Hirata was mounted on the posts."

Dawn gilded the rolling hills along State Road 800, and Jun's eyes opened.

Ghosts were supposed to be night creatures, so far as he knew, and it wasn't like he'd been murdered at daybreak or anything, so why he awoke at each dawn was a mystery to him. But he could guess why he awoke each morning on the steel T-post which had held first Kuebiko and then his own corpse.

He slid down from the pole with practiced ease and looked about. It was a long walk up 800 to reach the town, but there were no other options available to him. Teleportation did not seem to be a perk of the afterlife. If he wanted to see more of the trial, he would have to cover the ground himself.

A few snatches of mist still drifted over the road where it dipped, but it was a relatively clear morning. Jun kept well to the shoulder; though the morning drivers sped past him without braking or looking, he knew there was one who might see him, and he didn't want to startle her or make her swerve if she happened by.

It was a long distance to cover between dawn and the opening of court, and when he arrived the trial was already in session.

Hollie Madison was in the witness's chair again, her hands folded tightly in her lap. She was speaking mechanically, like the day before. "No, once I realized he was—I mean, I felt for a pulse, and there was nothing. And it was obvious there wouldn't be one, the way he looked, I only did it to be certain. And then I didn't touch him or anything else until the police arrived."

"Thank you, Dr. Madison," said the prosecuting attorney. "I have no further questions for you now."

Her eyes widened and she looked directly at him, her face breaking from its mask. "But—but I told you . . ."

The prosecutor shook his head, a tight little movement. "Not now, Dr. Madison."

But the judge was curious. "Is there something you wish to add, Dr. Madison?"

"The crows," she said breathlessly, looking between the prosecutor and Judge Fieldhouse. "The crows can identify the murderers."

There was a moment of awkward silence, as if the room were waiting for her to grin and admit the joke, but she did not.

When no one spoke, Hollie continued. "Crows can recognize human faces and can associate particular individuals with threat. Moreover, it's been amply demonstrated that crows can communicate this threat association, in effect warning other crows of a particular human who represents danger. I can supply corroborative material if the court wishes. Even though Dr. Hirata was working with wild crows, he had years of relationship with them over multiple generations, and it stands to reason that if a human broke into their research playground, destroyed all their toys and caches of food, and then killed the man they'd known all their lives, they'd perceive that human as a threat."

The prosecutor looked embarrassed, and he avoided the defending attorney's eyes. Judge Fieldhouse, with years of practice on the bench, kept her face mostly neutral. "And you want us to bring a crow to testify?"

"You accept the evidence of animals all the time," Hollie said. "Dogs report drugs or bombs or cadavers, and people are convicted on their evidence."

"Those dogs are specially trained and their reliability is independently assessed before and while their evidence is accepted," Judge Fieldhouse replied evenly. "These crows don't have any—there'd be no control group, I guess you'd say. Nothing to compare to."

"They were gathered all around Jun when I found him," Hollie said, her words rushing together. "They weren't—they didn't pick at his body, like they would have roadkill or something. They had assembled around him, viewing him as a conspecific." She amended her language to the layman's terms the court might understand. "They were treating him as one of their own!"

"I'm sorry, Dr. Madison, but there is no precedent for accepting the evidence of a bird in a murder trial," said Judge Fieldhouse. "Thank you for your testimony. The defense may now examine the witness."

Hollie left the room with a quickened stride, her face crumpling as she fought back tears. Jun looked after her, wanting to follow but knowing he would be useless. He could only watch her cry, and that helped neither of them.

He had not known the crows had assembled around him. That was very interesting.

The attorneys were directed to make their final statements, and the prosecutor's frustration was clear. Hollie's plea about the birds had emotionally weakened his case, which was a long shot in the first place. Most of the so-called activists who had admitted to being present were there for the thrill more than the cause and had also been drunk or under less-legal influences. None of them could reliably testify, even for a barter of dropped charges, to seeing their leader Everett Stapleton actually murder Dr. Hirata.

"So it is very possible that Dr. Hirata was still alive when my client left the scene, just as he has always maintained and as you have heard eyewitness Jeremy Reinbach corroborate. It is possible Dr. Hirata was killed by another, undiscovered murderer—perhaps someone who saw the fire and came to loot equipment. My client maintains that while he did destroy property and equipment, his motivation was to render the research facility useless for the exploitation of animals, not to take human life. It is only the most circumstantial of evidence which places him before you today."

Jun turned and looked at Everett, sitting mildly and proudly at the defendant's table. Protect the exploited animals, yes, and make a name for himself. Garner fame and attention and groupies for leading the fight against a better understanding of animals' abilities and public education to advocate for their welfare. Everett's motivation lay as much in the admiring coeds awed by an idealistic battle against an evil establishment as in any concern for animal welfare. It was probably true, Jun thought, that Everett had not gone to the station with the intention of killing him, but high on his followers' enthusiasm and zeal, he had gone too far, first striking Jun and then knocking him down and kicking him, stomping him, crushing face and bone.

Circumstantial evidence. Jun remembered it all, remembered it too clearly. But no one would hear him.

"That bird thing made us sound desperate," the prosecutor whispered to a suited man beside him. "They'll never convict."

They didn't.

⁓

Whenever an elephant died, other elephants gathered from miles around to mourn together. Jun had seen haunting video of an exhausted dolphin carrying her dead calf, other dolphins trailing respectfully on either side. Crows also held funerals for their dead where birds from beyond the deceased bird's family assembled and observed the dead, watching for hours in a sort of wake.

Jun hadn't known the crows had come near the burning building to gather around his staked corpse. If what Hollie had said was true, then he was flattered and humbled.

And Hollie might have been right about the birds and Stapleton. Crows remembered human faces and they could, to put it in anthropomorphic terms, hold long grudges. They neither forgave nor forgot. It was quite likely the station crows remembered Stapleton, and likely they would communicate a warning about him to other crows.

Too bad they couldn't warn other humans.

Jun shoved hard at a stack of legal files on the public defender's table, but without careful focus he managed only to dislodge two sheets, which wafted gently to the floor in a manner nothing at all like the mess he'd wanted. No one noticed.

Affecting the material world required careful concentration, he'd learned, and his anger left him helpless. He kicked at a couple chairs, futilely, and then passed out of the emptying courtroom.

A reporter was snapping a few photos on his phone to accompany the obligatory concluding story. The activism angle had given the case more journalistic legs than an ordinary murder, but it would not be headlining. If only Jun could speak to the reporter himself, give an interview—that would make headlines. Or put the reporter in a hospital for observation.

He thought of Sophie—once afraid of her hallucinations, now unable to talk about seeing ghosts. Could she have helped, somehow? Testified on Jun's behalf? No, the court was no more likely to admit as witness a newly-minted medium with a history of head trauma than a crow, even if Sophie could risk the publicity as she waited for the Wade Freeburn Wildlife Prize to be decided.

Jun left the courthouse, purposeless. He'd thought the trial was the reason for his remaining, and now it was ended. His murderer was free, and he had nowhere to go.

He supposed he could return to the wildlife center and quietly assist Sophie for . . . ever, he supposed. The animals who could perceive him saw him as something different, so maybe he could help without habituating them to humans. It wasn't how he'd planned to spend the afterlife, but in lieu of any other offer . . .

There was a knot of people about an ambulance and police car, lights flashing. Jun caught just a glimpse of Hollie's frightened face before the crowd shifted, and he started toward it. Then there was a slam of a car door and the police car started away, moving slowly. Were the police taking her home? But no, that was her car, being photographed with a measuring stick marking the distance between the bumper and curb. What had happened?

"He was one of the defense witnesses," someone said beside Jun. Jun looked at him, but the man didn't bother to lower his voice; he didn't know anyone was eavesdropping. He continued to the woman beside him, "She was one of the prosecuting witnesses. That's going to be ugly. Assault with a car? Pretty sure that's a deadly weapon."

Jun stared. Hollie would never. She *wouldn't*.

He recognized one of the young men standing nearby, photographing the policeman measuring from the curb. He was one of Everett's groupies, one who hadn't been called for the defense. The man turned and went to a parked car, dropping into the driver's seat, and Jun followed through the door, reading over the man's shoulder as he began uploading the photo onto social media.

Minutes after animal rights activist Everett Stapleton is cleared of charges, university researcher Hollie Madison is arrested for allegedly striking a defense witness with her car. You see what we're fighting? They don't want justice for animals or people. Donate now.

"You rotten—son of—*Kono yarou!*" No words seemed sufficient except his grandfather's reliable swearing. Jun made a grab for the phone but succeeded only in fumbling it from the youth's hands. The young man cursed his clumsiness and retrieved the phone, shutting it off and pocketing it.

Even if Jun could take the phone, he could not manage the fine motor skills of the keyboard to delete the post. He clenched his fists with infuriatingly little effect and shouted obscenities at the man, who adjusted the seat and turned on the radio.

A crow called, its voice harsh against Jun's fury, and he turned. Everett Stapleton was leaving the courthouse, flanked by several of his lieutenants. The young man left the car and jogged toward them, unwittingly trailing Jun. "I got it," he said, showing Everett the phone's screen.

The crow called again, and Jun noticed there were a number of birds in the few desultory trees about the parking lot.

Everett scanned the photo and message, and he grinned. "Eat that, bitch."

A black shape plunged out of a tree and swooped toward Everett, screeching. He jerked backward and shielded his face but the bird rose smoothly without touching him, squawking.

"Now they're after you," another activist said. "Like that *Birds* movie. Hey," he shouted after the crow, "don't you know he's on your side?"

The bird flew away and settled on a branch, silent. The other birds flapped and rustled and remained where they were.

Jun rode home with Everett, sitting in the back seat and looking from Everett to the driver as they laughed and swore and blew off the stress of the trial. Jun considered attempting to seize control of the car's steering wheel or brakes, sending Everett and his supporter into oncoming traffic, but the thought of saddling some innocent with their deaths stopped him. Everett deserved to die for his murder of Jun and his attack on Hollie, but the other drivers did not deserve a traumatic accident.

It was only fifteen minutes or so to Everett's apartment, and he slammed the car door with a wave and a promise to see his friend later. Jun followed him into the house.

Everett puttered through the apartment, trailing Jun as he checked over several houseplants and scowled at the enormous pile of mail on the kitchen table. He opened the fridge, swore, and then began scooping cartons and boxes into the trash. Apparently whoever had watered his plants and picked up his mail had not monitored the contents of the fridge. He filled the kitchen trash and then set the bag, loosely tied, in the corridor outside his door.

Jun drifted around the apartment, feeling peevish. If he couldn't have justice, he could have revenge—and if he couldn't have revenge, he could at least make Everett miserable. He found two rolls of toilet paper in the small bathroom and, concentrating, managed to maneuver both into the open toilet bowl. They immediately began wicking water into misshapen soggy messes, and he grinned.

In the open kitchen and living room, Everett had answered the phone. Jun went in to listen to the conversation.

"Jeremy stepped off the curb and got tagged by that Madison woman. His timing was good, he didn't get more than bruised—but it should be pretty easy to argue that either she was crying, so reckless driving, or that she meant to hit him, so assault. Whichever way it goes, that should be some good cash with a civil suit. Plus, it makes us the good guy in the David versus Goliath media picture."

He paused for a second and then laughed. "I know, right? She was a total windfall, that's for sure. We're going to file a suit for defamation of character, based on her assertion that the birds could recognize me as a murderer. It'd be hard to prove, but with her crazy bird talk we can make enough bad publicity that the university will pay just to shut us up. And she'll never work in academia again."

Jun clenched his fists, and his voice came out a guttural snarl. "You leave Hollie out of this."

Everett didn't hear him. "Plus there's the book deal, and we sign the contract Monday, so that's basically done. And marketing is already talking about a tour, you know, talk shows and appearance fees. All in all, it was a rough ride and I sure didn't appreciate the state's room and board, but it's all going to be worth it. There's a lot of money in being a controversial figure, you know?"

Jun swung at Everett and his fist passed through the laughing murderer's neck. It was no use; successful interaction with the material world lay in careful mental effort, and facing Everett ruined all his concentration.

"Thanks, man." Everett stretched, examined his wrist for a handcuff chafe, and then turned toward the windows. "Hold on, I can barely hear you. There's a mess of birds outside, some migration group or something." He went to the window.

Jun had hardly noticed the raucous cawing until Everett mentioned it.

Everett still had the phone to his ear. "Yeah, crows. I guess they really are on to me." He raised his voice in mock terror. "Oh, no, the crows are gonna tattle on me!"

Jun looked out the window at the birds, swarming the trees along the street. Some wore the plastic ID tags the university had used to monitor the wild population, but others did not.

"No, it's cool, I gotta go. Jeremy's got to stay in the hospital as long as he can, to make the driving thing stick, but the rest of us are going out to celebrate. Call me tomorrow, but not early." Everett clicked a button to end the call and dropped the phone on his couch.

Jun watched the birds for a moment. Perhaps they were just a migration group, as Everett had said, but outside of town seemed a more likely gathering place for them.

Everett's cry of dismay echoed in the bathroom, and Jun smiled smugly, pleased with his petty victory.

Jun awoke on his stake, arms flung wide, head lolling loosely to one side. Sunlight slanted over him and shone iridescent in the feathers of the dark bird sitting on his upturned elbow.

The bird blinked at him, oilslick feathers gleaming, and croaked a greeting. Then it launched into the air, flying off to join a few other dark birds crying as they winged westward.

Jun wriggled free and started after them.

Sophie arrived early, as he knew she would, which meant he could speak with her without potentially entrapping her in front of the wildlife center volunteers. He never meant to trouble her or put her at social risk by making her repeat her "hallucinations."

Nor did he mean to frighten her, but apparently she didn't expect to see him. She flipped on the lights and leaped backward at the sight of him. "Gah! Jun! What are you doing here?" She began to giggle, embarrassed at herself but unable to stop. "You scared me. Like I'd seen a ghost."

Jun gave her his best skeptical look.

"Give me a break," she protested. "You've never just been in the middle of the room, lurking. You always came to the door."

"Only while I had to pretend," he said. "Now I can save time."

"Creepy," she said. "But I'm glad to see you. I thought—I thought maybe you weren't coming back."

"I hoped . . . The trial ended."

She sobered. "I saw. I'm sorry."

"I'm not content to let Everett Stapleton walk away after killing me. And he's going to destroy Hollie's career and her life, and he's got a book deal, and—I won't have it."

She nodded. "So, what happens now?"

"I thought I was staying to see the trial finished, but now I think I stayed because I have work to do. And he is my work."

Sophie's eyes widened. "You're going to haunt him? Or something ghosty like that?"

"Not directly. He can't perceive me like you can. So I'll need your help."

"What, to tell him you're mad? He's not going to be impressed with me just saying stuff." Sophie shook her head firmly. "And I'm not putting a bullet into his brain so you can tell him yourself, not even if he deserves it."

"No, nothing like that. I just need you to promote Annabel a bit."

One corner of her mouth quirked ruefully. "I'd love to promote Annabel, and the wildlife center, and all kinds of things, but it takes money to make money, I've found."

"If you go out to East Groen Street and look beneath the third bush from the coffee shop, you'll find a few twenties. Everett had cash in his wallet when he went home last night."

Sophie regarded him with amazement. "You can burgle?"

"Only sort of, and only for this cause," he said. "But I have few moral compunctions where Everett's concerned."

"No, I didn't mean—it just hadn't occurred to me, what you could do," she said. "Weird."

"Manipulating objects is hard," he said, "but there's enough there to get you on a decent Goodwill shopping binge and get us started. Are you ready?"

Everett sprawled face-down on his bed, one arm dangling, a puddle of drool soaking into his pillow. He had managed to unfasten his jeans, exposing half his buttocks, but was otherwise still dressed in last night's clothes. Jun wondered if Everett and the bed might be inflammable with the excess of alcohol.

Jun sat and waited until Everett woke. The murderer scratched himself and stumbled into the bathroom, relieving himself in a long stream. Jun rose and placed a single black crow's feather on Everett's pillow.

Everett came back into the bedroom, cursing the excess of light. Jun looked at a stack of books—mostly heavy academic texts on biology, uncreased—and leaned over to give it a concentrated shove. The books collapsed with a heavy thud, and Everett flinched. Jun grinned.

Everett stared at the books a confused moment before he noticed the feather. He blinked and rubbed one eye, and then he made his way to the kitchen and glared at the empty coffeemaker. He reached for the box of individual plastic coffee packets and shook it out, scattering empty disposable plastic packaging over the counter.

"Worst conservationist ever," observed Jun.

Everett did not hear, of course. At last he cursed the empty box and the empty coffeemaker, fought into a clean pair of jeans and a shirt, and armored himself with sunglasses against the morning light. Jun followed him outside.

Everett was only a few steps from the coffee shop when the scarecrow lurched into the sidewalk. Everett recoiled, but whether from guilty horror or merely startled, Jun couldn't guess.

Sophie straightened from behind the scarecrow. "Oh, sorry! Just setting this out."

Everett stared at the scarecrow, pumpkin-headed and flannel-clad. It had not been hard to find thrift store clothing which suggested the clothes he had died in. The clothes he had been murdered in.

Everett scowled. "Stupid thing, blocking the sidewalk."

Sophie smiled pacifically. "Seasonal, you know. And it's for the wildlife center, after all. The manager said it would be all right to put it here."

A rusty *caw* sounded above them, and they both looked upward at the single crow perched on an overhead branch. A round white university ID tag flashed on its shoulder. "I guess the scarecrow isn't very good." Sophie giggled.

"Not really." Everett started forward again.

Sophie caught her breath, hand to mouth. "Hey, aren't you . . . Haven't we met? Stay—don't tell me—Stapleton? That's right! It was at the university, I think, one of the wildlife biology conferences. You were collecting interviews for a documentary or something."

Everett frowned at her, probably offended that she didn't immediately know the title. Sophie had not attended any of the several conferences Everett had graced with his bombastic presence, of course, but Jun rather suspected Everett was in the habit of forgetting many people who were not of immediate use either as groupies or for publicity. "Maybe," he said. "I was at Bowman quite a lot. Researching for *Blackbird*, among other things. And you are . . . ?"

"Sophie Jefferson, of the Bowman Wildlife Center. I'm sorry, I haven't been active in the community much lately; I had an accident earlier this year, was in a coma and then rehab for a while." She smiled apologetically.

"Yeah, Sophie. Nice to meet you. Er, again. Excuse me, please." Everett shoved past and went on to the coffee shop.

Jun went to join Sophie. He'd stayed away, not wanting to distract her as he faced Everett. "Good poker face."

"I did speech and debate in school."

Jun nodded toward the over-sized container of mums two dozen paces back on the sidewalk. "There's another twenty-seven dollars in there. He'd just shoved it in his pocket, easy to get to. You have a sticker design?"

"Better: Ashley has a cousin who does graphic design and is happy to get a tax deduction for his donation."

"Excellent. Now if you'll excuse me, I need to get to the coffee shop and watch Everett realize he can't pay for his order."

∽

Creating a viral campaign was easier with a ghost. Sophie would drop off posters and window clings, asking that they be left on the counter for a manager to review. At night, Jun would enter and hang them in the shop windows or on bulletin boards and counter fronts. The next day, everyone assumed someone else had approved and posted them.

And the campaign began to catch on of its own merit. The scarecrow and bird design from Ashley's cousin managed to be simultaneously cute and edgy, and word began to catch on about the injured crow who could count aloud. A bookstore owner asked Sophie to bring Annabel for a visit and told her she could sell t-shirts and other items to raise money. Sophie charged the shirts, crossing her fingers that they'd sell quickly enough to pay for themselves before the bill arrived.

Everett did not approve of the posters. "They say it's for wildlife rehabilitation and conservation," he observed loudly in the coffee shop, nodding toward the scarecrow and bird in the window, "but it's obviously just a cash grab. Putting a bird on display like that, exploiting it for tricks—that's disgusting."

The barrista had graduated the previous year from Bowman University and remembered the attack on the research station. "The bird can't fly," she said practically. "If she weren't doing educational programs with the center, she'd be dead."

"Maybe she should be dead, then," Everett snapped. "That's the natural run of things, survival of the fittest."

The line waiting to order went quiet. Everett might have been found not guilty, but *someone* had killed the university doctor, and no one else had been charged. The scarecrow motif played subtly on people's memory of the initial news coverage.

"This way, at least people are learning about the birds," someone said from the rear of the line. "Maybe they'll think twice about conserving energy or something now."

"I never knew crows were so smart," said one woman. "My kid wants to give his birthday money to the wildlife shelter. So I guess it's doing some good, after all."

"My little girl says she wants to grow up to be a scientist now, study bird intelligence," said a man with a tall steaming cup.

Everett wasn't a stupid man. He'd made his way down the celebrity path by reading and catering to trending public opinion, and he sensed he was losing ground in even indirectly advocating the death of an injured and intelligent crow. "I didn't mean she should be euthanized now, of course," he said. "I meant, maybe the resources spent on her and this promotional campaign could be better used elsewhere. Doesn't the wildlife center have other animals to feed and medicate? How can they justify four-color posters and t-shirts, then?"

He didn't wait for a rebuttal, snatching his venti and stalking toward the door. As he opened it and stepped into the October sunshine, a black feather fell over him and drifted onto the white plastic lid of his cup.

Everett looked up, and a trio of black birds gave rusty caws from a branch overhead.

∽

Jun found Everett sitting with two friends and fellow activists at a sidewalk table of the local vegan cafe. He took a seat in the empty fourth chair at their table.

"I'm just saying," said one with a blindingly white bandage on his temple, "that you've been weird lately. Jumpy."

That must be Jeremy. Hollie's hearing was next week. Jun clenched his fists hard, and the paper napkin weighted by a fork before him fluttered a little despite the opposing breeze.

"He's right," said another. Frank, Jun thought. "It's all over, but you're worse now than during the trial. What's wrong with you?"

Everett wasn't looking at them. "Those birds," he said. "They're watching me."

The others turned to a wire drooping beneath the weight of a dozen crows. Most wore university ID tags. None were looking at the table. "Really, man? Come on, Everett."

He shook his head. "They're watching me. All the time. My apartment, out here, everywhere. And there's more of them all the time." He swallowed, his eyes still on the birds. "They're gathering."

Frank turned to look at them. "Not much of a gathering. Or a murder, I guess it is."

"Flock," snapped Everett. "Only poets call them a murder."

Still, thought Jun, *the term had to come from somewhere.*

"But they're flocking around me, more and more."

Jeremy snorted. "If this is a joke, dude, you can drop it. We get it. You do a good crazy act."

"I'm not joking, man!" Everett's eyes looked as if he'd had his espresso as a tall. "They've started to bring things."

"What do you mean, bring things?"

"Scissors, needles, clips." Everett dropped his voice, embarrassed to speak but needing to confide. "Weapons."

Jeremy looked as if he wanted to laugh but was afraid to. "Weapons, man? Seriously?"

"They use tools!" Everett jabbed a finger toward the crows. "You know what they can do, how they think—they use effin' tools!" He slammed his hand down on the table, making a spoon jump to the ground, and screamed.

Even Jun jerked back from the table as Everett leaped up, clutching his hand to his chest. Jeremy and Frank looked at each other and then at Everett, inexplicably cradling his hand and swearing. But then Everett turned on them and shoved his hand at them. "See? See what I mean?"

A tiny drop of red blood marked the exit point of the fishhook, barbed and glistening and snaked neatly through the flesh of Everett's palm.

Frank boggled. "Why was there a fishhook on the table? How does that even happen?"

"The crows put it there!" Everett snatched up the flatware from the table and hurled it, piece by piece, at the birds on the wire. They exploded into the air, screeching annoyance. "Get away from me! You freaking monsters! Keep away!"

"Everett, stop!" Jeremy jumped up and grabbed his arm. "Not here. Not in public. Let's talk about this."

"Get off me!" Everett shoved Jeremy away. "They're on to me, Jeremy. Like that bitch said. They're leaving feathers in my apartment, every day, and you see the fishhook." He flung another fork.

"Everett!" Frank was out of his seat now, too.

Everett drew away from both of them, turning back toward the cafe door. He made an inarticulate sound somewhere between a cry and a snarl and lurched forward to tear the scarecrow and bird logo poster from the window, ripping it in half and throwing it to the ground.

"Hey," said a waiter, coming outside. "What's going on here, friend?"

Everett swore viciously at him and stalked down the street, cradling his hand.

Neither Everett nor his friends had noticed the Bowman College student a few tables over pull her smart phone for a few awed photos of the celebrity activist, nor her subsequent jaw-hanging recording of his screaming attack on the birds. It wouldn't be long now; Everett's crumbling persona would not be able to maintain the charm which had carried him thus far. His activist days were coming to a close, along with the glamour and attention he craved.

Jun laced his fingers behind his head and smiled.

⁓

The television replayed the footage, shaky but clear, and paused on Everett's face twisting mid-obscenity. Block text at the bottom of the screen read, *Video allegedly shows animal rights activist attacking birds at outdoor cafe.*

"We caught Jeremy Reinbach, one of Everett Stapleton's closest associates and a witness for the defense at Stapleton's trial for murder three weeks ago. Let's hear what Reinbach had to say about this incident."

Jeremy, too-white bandage brandished over his temple, looked worried and hurried. "Well, Everett's been under a lot of stress, you know? That university doctor at the trial said the birds would see him as a murderer, would recognize—that is, not that he committed any murder, but even the suggestion . . . He's been under a lot of pressure, and she should never have said that." He licked his lips. "That's all, no further comment."

The local news anchor appeared again. "Everett Stapleton did not return our request for a statement. And now, let's go to sports."

Jun smiled and scratched Annabel's head. She rubbed her beak along his forefinger. He let her for a moment, and then he used both hands to set a folded notepaper against the computer monitor. "This is for Sophie," he told the bird. "I think you're going to have to deliver it. I might not . . . be available."

Annabel took the paper in her beak and adjusted it with a foot.

"No, no, for Sophie. Not curious birds." He rubbed Annabel's head again. "You be a good girl. Get that grant money so Sophie can take care of you and everyone else." He'd seen today's email asking Sophie for another interview with the Wade Freeburn Prize jury, about the local enthusiasm she was generating for wildlife care. That was a good sign.

Everett Stapleton was ruined, or at least likely suffering a breakdown. That was good enough for Jun. He yawned, sleepy as every night, though his unreal body shouldn't tire, and lay his head down on Sophie's desk. It did not matter where he went to sleep; he awoke every morning on Kuebiko's post at the research station. But perhaps, this time, he would not.

⌒⌘⌒

Everett slammed the brakes and skidded the car on the gravel road. "I'll show you," he muttered. "I'll show them all. No stupid birds are going to ruin my life, going to destroy my work. You're trying to make me look bad? How's that going to work out when you're dead, huh?"

He seized the Mossberg 500 from the seat beside him and jerked back the bolt to shove shells into the loading gate. He'd borrowed the gun—he'd ask Frank later, but he would have said yes—and the birdshot Frank used for skeet competitions. When the loading tube was full, he kicked open the door and got out.

The field leading to the burned out building was covered in birds. Hundreds—no, thousands—gathered in a massive migratory group and darkened the ground. He swung the shotgun to his shoulder and sighted. An activist and vegan, he hadn't handled a gun much, but it wasn't so different from *Call of Duty*.

But he hesitated, finger on the trigger. If he fired from here, he'd hit a few birds with the edge of the blast, and the rest would escape into the air. He needed to be closer, needed to fire directly into the center of the flock, to kill as many as possible.

He gripped the shotgun by the barrel and started forward. The sagging barbed wire fence didn't present much of an obstacle; he leaned the shotgun barrel-up against the post and climbed the strands like a rope ladder. Safely on the ground again, he collected the shotgun and started slowly toward the birds.

They were muttering to themselves, speaking in strange and unhurried calls. He wondered briefly how much they understood of each other. How much they were communicating. How much they were conspiring.

They let him draw quite near, stupid birds. *So much for intelligence.* He raised the shotgun to his shoulder.

Something struck him hard in the side of his head. He ducked instinctively, and a black bird swooped away from him. He put a hand to his ear and felt warm liquid.

He swore and jerked the shotgun up again, but another bird dove at him. He swung the gun toward it, whether to shoot or club he wasn't sure, but yet another bird came at him from the other side, seizing a beakful of cheek skin and twisting savagely.

Everett yelped and whirled, flailing with his arm to protect his head, and the field took flight.

He raised the gun, squinting, but he couldn't hope to aim; there were too many, in all directions. But he could scare them off. He pulled the trigger and the stock kicked hard against his collarbone—he hadn't braced it properly. Swearing, he worked the bolt to reload, but birds descended upon him, shrieking, biting, pecking, clawing, twisting.

The car! He had to get inside the car, or they would kill him. He ducked his head, swinging the shotgun like a flail, and turned back toward the road. He ran, stumbling and bent over, and they tore at his hands and forearms and clothes. He fell, and he clawed at the ground to pull himself up and forward, tufts of dead grass clinging to him.

He hit the fence before he saw it, and the barbs caught at him. He flung himself onto the wire, pushing off with the gun against the ground, and scrabbled with his feet for a toehold. His foot caught on something which gave.

He heard the gun's roar first, before he actually registered the white-hot fire over his throat and jaw. In numb horror he reached for his neck, felt a mash of blood and pulp. A bird struck him, tore a bit of his flesh away.

He twisted, slapped grasping birds away, fell, caught himself on barbed wire. He screamed, and his voice was a broken and raspy thing, a terrified caw. He lunged, was brought up short, slid between strands. Crows struck his neck, his jaw, his face, his ears, his eyes. He fell, screaming, and a crow bit at his tongue.

It was the next day before police received a report of a car on a spur off State Road 800 and a dead man near it. They found him strung in the barbed wire, arms extended, head lolling, a specter of blood and shattered flesh. On either side of him, and on his flopping head and shoulders, sat crows, undisturbed by the monstrous scarecrow.

Waking from His Master's Dream

Katherine Marzinsky

When Rosa entered Vicente's hospital room, she was greeted by a picture of obscene contrast. Her older brother lay like a filthy shadow against the sterile white of the bed sheets. A living scarecrow, whose body shed bits of straw with each breath, sat hunched in the chair beside him.

"Get out of here," Rosa growled at the scarecrow. She shoved it aside and tossed her tangled curls over her shoulder.

Vicente's eyes cracked open, letting the raw yolk of his gaze spill out.

"S-Strel?" Vicente murmured, reaching for the scarecrow. "Where . . . are we?"

"You're in the hospital," Rosa said, interrupting. "In Cielotriste. Your appendix exploded. All the shit in your soul leaked out into the rest of your body."

At the sight of his sister, Vicente's eyebrows rose into his overgrown bangs; the heart monitor began to beep an anxious staccato.

The scarecrow named Strel stared at the newcomer.

"Rosa," Vicente grumbled.

"Vicente."

"Get her out of here, Strel. I don't want to talk to her."

Rosa pulled a cigarette lighter out of her purse.

"Either you make that thing leave, or I will, Vicente. I didn't come all the way down here, after all these years, just to be chased away by your dumb, ass-kissing *ficción*."

Ficción. The deceptively simple name given to a fictional character brought to life by its author. The process, known as Solidification, had originated in Rosa and Vicente's home city of Cielotriste, but it had quickly spread, engulfing states, leaping seas and borders. The Fabulist Party said Solidification was like the miracle of birth; the Realists likened it to a dangerous heathen ritual. These days, political debates between the parties often ended in violent riots.

Vicente sighed in tired resignation and told Strel to wait in the hall. Rosa took the seat the scarecrow had previously occupied.

"So," Rosa began, her voice the temperature of the water on the bedside tray, "you're still wandering around with that stupid straw-man of yours?"

"Yes," Vicente replied with equal coldness, studying the IV line running into his wrist. "He's my *hermano de tinta.* Why wouldn't I be?"

"I'm just a little surprised." Rosa crossed one leg over the other. "I thought you'd have scrapped him and run off with some new, half-baked story by now." She met Vicente's eyes. "After all, that's what you did with us, your real brother and sister."

Vicente looked away.

". . . I wasn't ready to handle all that nonsense."

"We're nonsense?" Rosa's eyes widened. "Your family is nonsense? And just what do you think that damn scarecrow is?"

"I needed time for myself."

"All you ever think about is yourself." Rosa uncrossed her legs and braced her palms against her thighs. "Mamá and Papá didn't raise us to act that way. Do you know how ashamed they'd be if they knew how you abandoned us? Abandoned your life and their memory? Luis is almost a teenager now, and he doesn't remember anything except Mamá's coffin and you walking away."

"Shut up." Vicente knotted his fists around the bed sheets and squeezed until his veins bulged like worms. "You don't have any idea what you're talking about. You don't know me; you never knew me."

"Who does then?"

Feeling the pain rising from the IV needle on the back of his hand, Vicente let go of the sheets. He closed his eyes for a moment, and then shrugged the best he could in his cocoon of linens, gauze, and plastic tubing.

"Strel's the only one. Not like you'd ever ask him though."

"That's bullshit, Vicente. Your scarecrow can't even talk."

"Maybe you just don't know how to listen." Vicente turned his head to the wall. Wind began to rattle the panes of the window. "I'm not going to talk about this anymore. I'm sick, Rosa. If you just came here to make me feel like crap, then leave."

"You'd love that, wouldn't you? But then who would pay for all this? Do you even think about things like that?"

A nurse, her face wrinkled by too many night shifts and infectious tragedies, stepped into the room.

"Is everything all right in here?" the nurse asked. "I saw your fictional friend sitting out in the hall."

"Señora?" Rosa asked before Vicente could reply. "Isn't there some rule about allowing *ficciones* in the hospital rooms? Doesn't it agitate the patients?"

"Oh no, Señora. Quite the opposite. In fact, we've got two authors and twice as many of their *ficciones* on staff. They're extremely useful, especially upstairs. You'd be amazed at what a well-crafted character can do to help people."

Vicente flashed a weak, but triumphant smirk at Rosa.

"And people wonder why this country's going to hell . . ." Rosa stood up, resisting the urge to reach into her purse for a cigarette. "This is what happens when the Fabulists run the show."

Her mouth hanging open like a landed tarpon, the nurse looked from Vicente to Rosa.

"Um . . . Señora?" The nurse raised one finger and tried to inch her way to Vicente's IV bag. "Would you like to go down to the cafeteria and get a cup of coffee? I have some things I have to take care of here.

Medication. Dressings. Cleaning up. When you get back we'll let you speak to the doctor again concerning your brother's condition."

Rosa nodded and exited, heading for the elevator.

As Rosa neared the metal doors, a nurse with features far too perfect to be anything but a *ficción* stepped out. Even more telling than the nurse's unnatural perfection was her form. Rather than a human, the nurse was a tall, anthropomorphized poodle, with hypoallergenic curls as clean and fluffy as newborn clouds, and eyes like melted chocolate. Although she stank of ink and morphine, the poodle's face was devoid of wrinkles and her eyes were unsoiled by tearstains. Her uniform, a white skirt and hat, looked like something from the last century; her badge marked her as a citizen of the pediatric oncology ward.

Frowning distastefully, Rosa looked the creature over, from floppy ears to rubber-soled shoes. She stepped in front of the *ficción* to block its path.

"Why do you think you should be here?" Rosa asked.

The nurse blinked and did an awkward sort of half-bow.

"Señora? What do you mean? I'm a nurse; I work here. Upstairs."

"Yes, but why isn't a real human doing your job?"

"Oh . . ." the nurse smiled and pointed to her ID badge, where her author's name was listed above her own. "Well, I'm here because my author really wanted to help people, but she can't stand to look into sick children's eyes. She likes to say I was born of a compromise between what she fears and what she desires."

"I see." Rosa scowled and nodded as if her neck were made of wood. "Very noble."

"Thank you." The fictional poodle's tail began to wag, and she stepped forward as if to continue down the hallway.

Rosa blocked her path again.

"I have a neighbor." Rosa narrowed her eyes into tiger-fanged coals. "She spent four years and her life's savings on nursing school. Now she's unemployed and in debt because she can't find any job openings."

"I . . ." the *ficción* faltered and glanced at the nurse's station in the distance, "I'm sorry to hear that."

"Yeah." Rosa stepped out of the way to let the nurse past. "I'm sure you are."

∽

While Rosa and Vicente met with the doctor, Strel dozed fitfully in the waiting room. Night had fallen; before drifting into sleep, all the scarecrow had seen through the window was a galaxy of parking lot headlights. All he had heard was the droning argument between an air-conditioning vent and a snack machine in the opposite corner. Now, his head was filled with a familiar nightmare, scraps of a narrative Vicente had penned, the narrative from which Strel had been born so many years ago.

∽

Strel was alone.

Looking to the sky, the scarecrow zipped his coat and shivered in the wind.

Too much time spent guarding that muddy field had left Strel's boots reeking of mildew. Toads slumbered in his pant pockets and the hay in his chest had wilted over his ribs. He had become ill with silence.

Below, gust-afflicted October leaves dragged along the ground. Above, the crows began to reel, screaming and croaking, silhouetted in the sky like shadow puppets on a mausoleum wall.

The creatures shrieked and wheeled; they dove at Strel with malice in their wings.

In a state of panic, Strel pulled a rusty, old scythe from the mud. He almost lost his grip on the tool as he lifted it, causing the scythe's wicked blade to topple forward and lop away the leaves of a cornstalk he was supposed to be protecting. Panting, the scarecrow hefted the scythe once again. He hunched beneath it, hoping it could protect him from those feathered dirges.

Strel looked on in horror as the largest of the birds hopped toward him in its gawky, ominous way. Perched atop a fallen pumpkin stem, the bird began to speak to him in a human voice. It reprimanded him for selfishly guarding the cornfield. It shamed him. It made him feel like an incompetent child. The bird lurched forward and flushed its tail feathers each time it thought it was making an important point.

Strel dropped the scythe and ran from the eloquent raven, past the dilapidated barn, into the golden woods beyond. Struggling against a guilty wind, Strel walked away from all that he once was.

∼

With a silent snore, Strel flailed awake, surprising a sad-eyed woman in the waiting room, and causing her to drop her knitting needles. The scarecrow knelt to pick up the needles, remembering how he had cradled Vicente when, moaning with pain and clutching his side, the man had collapsed and dropped his guitar. Written as a mute, Strel could not call for help. He had been forced to wave his arms by the side of a country road. When no cars had stopped, Strel had dragged Vicente to a bus stop and laid him on a bench caked with bird droppings. He had displayed the change from Vicente's pockets to make it clear that they were not begging. Finally, a charitable commuter had gotten the message and called an ambulance.

Now, however, Strel felt spasms of regret within his burlap-clad ribcage. After witnessing the vicious reunion between Vicente and Rosa, he had begun to wonder if it had been a mistake to nod "yes" to the admitting office's questions about family members and emergency contacts. He had begun to wish that Vicente's old address and phone number had not been present on his story's first manuscript, the only document from the old days his author had kept.

Rosa listened to Vicente's doctor with the taste of burnt coffee on her tongue. In addition to his appendix, Vicente had shown signs of anemia, malnourishment, and liver inflammation, most likely due to alcohol abuse. Still, he was going to make a full recovery, and would likely be released from the hospital within a few days. Her brother would, however, be weak for some time; he would need antibiotics and a careful eye.

In short, Vicente would have to return home with Rosa.

The day Vicente was released from the hospital, the nurses insisted he be brought out to the parking lot in a wheelchair.

"But I can walk just fine," Vicente objected, moving to stand up. "I feel fine now."

The nurse pushed him back into the wheelchair.

"Hospital policy," she said with a pre-packaged smile and a shrug.

Vicente frowned as the nurse wheeled him out to the parking lot, where he found Strel holding his backpack and guitar case. A few minutes later, Rosa pulled up in her car.

Vicente was positive that of all the cars in the world, there was none more disgusting than his sister's. It was a rusted abomination the color of dried blood. Its passenger seat was frozen in place, mashing Vicente's knees into a glovebox that had never been opened.

In Vicente's eyes, Rosa herself had taken on the qualities of her car. Tired, older than her years, bitter like warped plastic, his sister was a shadow of her former self. Not that she had ever been anything great to begin with. Even if she thought otherwise. From schoolwork to politics to church, she had used every opportunity to prove she was better than him. She'd diminished everything he had ever been proud of, his songs and poems. Rosa had not embraced life in creativity, as he had. For that, Vicente felt she deserved to rot in her martyrdom. He just wished he hadn't been forced to see it.

Vicente rested his forehead against the window.

"Where are we going?" he sighed, his coffee-bean eyes scrutinizing the horizon, the fading cityscape and doleful marshes. "I don't recognize this road."

"Of course you don't," Rosa said. "You've never been here."

"Fine." Vicente manipulated one foot onto the dashboard. "Whatever." He peeked into the backseat where Strel sat patiently. "Is this going to take long? I thought we were going straight home."

"Maybe." Rosa finagled a cigarette from her pocket with one hand and held it between her lips. She dug into the center console for a lighter.

Vicente rolled down his window and wrinkled his nose.

"That's a terrible habit," he scolded. "Since when do you smoke?"

"Don't talk to me about terrible habits, Vicente." Rosa took a deep drag on the cigarette; she blew the smoke into her brother's face. "Yours is sitting in my back seat."

Strel leaned forward in response to the acknowledgment and set a hand on the back of Rosa's headrest.

"Tell that *thing* not to touch me," Rosa hissed, lurching forward.

"Don't talk about Strel like that."

"Get its hand off of me." Rosa recoiled further from Strel's innocent motion.

Vicente slammed his hand against the interior of the car door.

"*He* has a name!"

"So did you." Rosa reached backward and ground her cigarette into Strel's fingers. The scarecrow jerked away. "Tell me what happened to that. Tell me how you ran away into an escapist wasteland with that thing. Tell me how you left me and Luis to fend for ourselves while you sacrificed yourself to an idol of your own writing."

Strel cradled his burnt hand and looked to Vicente.

"Let us out," Vicente demanded, his voice deepening to a furious growl.

Rosa kept her eyes on the road.

"No. You're not well."

"Let us the hell out of this car, Rosa."

"No. We're going somewhere you need to go."

Vicente's eyes flicked from the car door to the speedometer. He fell into a fuming silence.

As Strel tried to ignore the sting of his burn, the car passed through the gates of a cemetery. Lilies swayed along ashen tombstones. Tires flattened gravel. The odor of Vicente's perspiration mingled with Rosa's perfume.

Vicente's breath came in quiet, shallow bursts as the car slowed.

"Take me home, Rosa."

"No," Rosa replied, parking the car beside a spigot. "Besides, didn't you tell me the apartment wasn't your home? Before you ran away, on the day of Mamá's funeral?"

"I want to leave."

"No."

"Rosa! I don't want to be here!" Vicente struck the door again. "You just said I'm not well. You think this is going to help me feel better?"

"You need to be here." Rosa removed the key from the ignition, lit up another cigarette, and she tossed the previous butt into the backseat. "This is your life, Vicente."

"This is no place for Strel."

"You're the one who insisted he come with us."

"I wasn't going to just leave him at the hospital! I thought we were going straight home. Rosa, please . . ."

Ignoring her brother's words, Rosa swung open her door and circled around to the trunk. She removed a bouquet of chrysanthemums.

"Get out of the car." Rosa slammed the trunk. "And say a prayer for Mamá and Papá."

"No. I don't want to be here."

Rosa returned to the open driver's-side door and met Vicente's eyes. She took an exasperated drag on her cigarette.

"We're not going to leave this cemetery until you come with me, Vicente. You can't live in denial forever."

"Rosa, this is insane."

"This is reality."

Vicente buckled his previously unfastened seatbelt and crossed his arms. He closed his eyes so he could not see Rosa's face.

"Piss off," he said.

After a few moments, Vicente heard the car door close and Rosa's footsteps retreat into the graveyard. He dared to open his eyes only when everything had fallen silent. He adjusted the rearview mirror so he could see Strel's face.

"Are you okay?" Vicente murmured to his character. "Did she burn you bad?"

Strel continued to cradle his burnt hand and trained his eyes on his author. A drowsy wind pushed clouds over the already-faint midday sun.

"What?" Vicente asked. "What're you looking at me like that for?"

Strel could not help but notice how exhausted his author looked. A peculiar sensation, similar to what he had felt with the hospital admitting staff, began to creep through the scarecrow. A restless itching like crickets and field mice. Strel could not say why, but he clambered forward and exited the car. He pulled open Vicente's door.

"Strel. Get back in the car. This place isn't for you. You don't have to see this."

Strel heard Vicente's plea as if in another language, some obscure cipher in which "X" meant "Y" and "stop" meant "go." He turned away.

Vicente watched helplessly as Strel followed the trail of footsteps Rosa had left in the mud.

Several dozen meters away, in front of an oppressive granite slab, Rosa knelt with her hand on the bouquet. Smoke curled above her head; twice her cigarette almost fell from between the pallid whispers of her prayer.

Strel crept forward and tried to brush the bouquet aside to better read the headstone, but Rosa's eyes flicked open before he could reach it. Bursting out of her piety like a prodded lion, she backhanded him.

"Don't touch that, *bazofia*!"

The blow flung Strel's slight form to the side. Rosa exhaled a draconic cloud of smoke.

"Rosa!" Vicente shouted, rushing forward.

The woman turned at Vicente's sudden appearance. Her hopes were dashed, however, when her brother ran to the scarecrow instead of her.

"So, you'll follow that thing out here," she sighed, "but you won't follow me?"

"Shut up." Vicente knelt in the mud and draped Strel's arm over his shoulder. "He's my brother."

"That isn't your brother, Vicente! Luis is your brother! And I'm your sister!" Rosa tossed her cigarette to the ground and stomped on it. She threw her hands into the air. "God, Vicente! Why won't you open your eyes?"

"Why?" Vicente snapped. "So I can look at a place like this?"

Rosa's face softened into something like stripped wire when she saw how tenderly her brother took the character's hand in his own. She sucked in a breath free of nicotine.

"I love you, Vicente," she rasped. "Don't you see that? If I didn't love you, it wouldn't bother me that you're such a pitiful bastard."

"Good for you." Vicente hoisted Strel to his feet. "I hope that makes you feel really holy, Rosa. I hope you have a lot to brag about on Sunday. You *love* your pitiful disgrace of a brother."

Rosa watched Vicente struggle under the weight of his own imagination, saw how pathetically her brother and his *ficción* cleaved to one another.

"Would you help me like that?" she asked. "If I fell?"

"I don't know."

"I would help you." Rosa paused and glanced at the headstone behind her. "I'm trying to help you."

"I don't care. I want to leave."

Strel pushed away from Vicente. He stumbled toward the headstone and stood motionless, reading the words engraved into it, the names and lifespans of Vicente's parents, unchangeable mortal facts written in stone. Both Vicente and Rosa watched in silence as the scarecrow cocked his head to the side.

Vicente swore under his breath and returned to the car.

Strel remained by the grave and prostrated himself before the headstone even amid his author's retreat, even as a flock of crows began to forage beside him. After a moment, the scarecrow's shoulders began to quake. When one of the dreadful birds tried to steal a flower from the bouquet, he gritted his teeth and waved it away.

Intrigued, Rosa sucked on one end of an unlit cigarette and watched Strel cry. For almost an hour, she stood running her tongue over the soggy paper and tobacco, pondering the void between her brother and the muted grief of his phantasm. She thought of the past, and she thought of the nurse at the hospital. At some point, Rosa realized that Strel had poured out enough illusory tears to kill a man of Vicente's stature. He had drained the well of human bereavement, dehydrated nonexistent veins running to a nonexistent heart.

And, still, the scarecrow continued to sob.

THE STRAW SAMURAI

Andrew Bud Adams

Okamiko was short, with short legs and short arms, and a head full of wild black hair that stuck out in every direction. Layers of dirt hid her clothes, which was all the better, since her kimono was a rice sack, her sash an old rope. She had no sandals, but went about barefoot. A bamboo stick was her playmate, weapon, and walking staff.

But she didn't travel far. In fact, she merely migrated between a series of close mountain villages, moving on to another when they drove her from the last. These were far away from any human settlements and named for the types of people who inhabited them: Inugami, the dog-people; Bakeneko, their cat-people rivals; Kitsune, the fox-people; Oni, the cow and pig people, who were all quite large; Kappa, the turtle-people, who lived close to the water; Tsuchigumo, the spider-people, whose village was most isolated; and so on. Okamiko belonged to none of them, though she wished she did.

The villagers scowled when she came, whispering that her human ancestors drove their ancestors away. They forbade their children from playing with her, which was the same as permission to tease and torment her.

Okamiko pretended teasing and torment were the same as playing.

She returned again and again, grateful for the torment, laughing when the children threw their scowls and their insults and their rocks. She swung her stick, batting the rocks back at them like a game, until she was convinced it was one. She was confused when the children, struck back and bleeding, ran crying. Their parents chased Okamiko away on paws, claws, and thundering hooves. One day's playtime ended with another long wait—and long walk—before the next.

She returned to Inugami, the dog-people, most often. They were the simplest and the kindest and the most playful of any village, and she'd had the most luck befriending them. She even thought she resembled a Dog herself, hairy as she was. Her human traits didn't seem to offend them as much, and maybe even endeared her to them, like a fascinating creature they would make their pet.

But unlucky things happened in their village when Okamiko came to visit. Children often got hurt playing with her, even without a game of rocks. Livestock were skittish. Shingles blew off roofs. Clay pots fell from tables and shelves. Treasures went missing from holes. The Dogs, with their keen senses, noticed the change in atmosphere and blamed Okamiko. In time, they rejected her, too, and began to treat her like the other villages did.

When Okamiko was alone, which was most of the time, she would talk to her only playmate, the bamboo stick. She called him Take, which means bamboo.

∾

Another day ended running from the villager's rakes. Laughing and out of breath, Okamiko collapsed in the mud and held Take close, agreeing that the villagers were getting better at their side of this game, and the two of them would have to try harder tomorrow. She thanked him for his help. He was the best teammate, and with some other stick, she would miss the rocks; then when they struck her, who would she cry to? Take told her the teams were uneven and before long she was shuddering again—not from laughter or to catch her breath, but from crying. She asked Take why the teams were uneven, why he was her only friend, but this time he had no answer. She fell asleep in a rice field, wrapped around her bamboo friend like a dog with its bone.

A rustling in the tall yellow stalks woke Okamiko. She heard it all around her, but when she opened her eyes she saw only the blue sky framed in grain. Her first thought was animals—regular animals who couldn't talk—because she was used to sharing her bed with them; but the rustling was too rhythmic. She sat up, using Take to stand.

The rustling stopped. Surrounding her were four workers, but now that they stared at her, she saw they weren't from any of the familiar villages. They had red faces with long, curved beaks, and their scaly red hands gripped bundles of grain. The rest of their bodies were covered in sleek black feathers, except for their feet, which were red and taloned like their hands. They wore colorful jackets, divided skirts, and conical hats like people, but were short, almost as short as Okamiko, as if they were children.

They stared a moment longer, appraising her, too, and then went back to work gathering stalks.

She watched them wide-eyed, afraid to move, afraid the work was a trick and they were crow-people who had spied her lying as if dead and come to peck out her eyes. The thought made her squint and look away, but she didn't move. They kept harvesting around her, and it was only when she was several yards in their wake that she stood taller and her expression changed. She cocked her head like a puppy, more curious than frightened, and yelped, "What are you doing?"

They didn't stop. One looked back at her, that curved red beak swiveling like a bloody sickle. She saw herself in its big round eye, saw how naked and plain she must look to them, but that only increased her curiosity, because they were not angry nor afraid.

"Who are you?" she asked.

They ignored her.

She watched them get smaller and their bundles get bigger. Then, overcome by her curiosity, she ran after them. "Hey!" she shouted. "Hey, talk to me! Please? No one will talk to me! Who are you? What are you doing out here? Why are you gathering the rice?"

They ignored her.

Almost in their midst again, she barked, "Hey, Crows!"

They didn't stop, but the one who had looked back said, in a voice sweeter and more feminine than Okamiko's, "We aren't Crows. We're Choughs."

"Is that a crow spirit?"

"No," said the girl Chough, still working. "A Crow is a crow-person and a Chough is a chough-person."

Okamiko didn't hear the capitals on "Crow" and "Chough" and twisted her lips in confusion, trying to understand.

The girl Chough sighed. "It's a bird. And we're Birds."

"I can *see* that," Okamiko said. "What are you doing out here? Stealing rice?"

"No," another Chough said, sounding like a boy. "We're stealing *straw.*"

"And we're stealing rice," a third Chough admitted, his voice cracking. "It's silly to throw it away, so long as we're taking the stalks."

"Why are you taking the stalks?" Okamiko asked.

The Choughs paused and looked at each other, their beaks swiveling back and forth as each took the other three in, apparently having a silent debate about whether or not to answer Okamiko's question. Or maybe they had no answer to her question, and this was the first they'd considered it.

She, too, used this time to consider, looking between them and the direction of the nearest village. This was an Oni field. To whom should she be loyal?

This could be her chance to earn the pig-people's trust and admiration; she could warn them that these silly Birds were stealing their rice. But why should she? Their children had been cruel to her, while these chough-children were polite . . . or at least had not thrown rocks at her, and seemed to have no intention of doing so. She looked to Take for advice, but he was silent, like a regular stick of bamboo.

The decision weighed on her, and she whined a bit, shuffling her feet and turning back and forth like a dog torn between two masters.

The Choughs' quiet counsel must have ended, because the girl suddenly said, "We're building a straw man."

Okamiko forgot her indecision. "A what?"

"A straw man."

Okamiko studied their impressive conical hats, realizing they were expertly woven from yellow stalks. "You make things with the straw?"

The children continued working, and Okamiko almost forgot to keep up. Bouncing in front of them to get a head start, and nearly laughing with enthusiasm, she said, "Why a straw man? What will you do with a straw man? Why not a straw woman? Have you made straw people before? It must not be for battle, because a straw man is easily knocked down. Is it to scare someone? How strange that Crows are stealing rice to make a scarecrow, when a scarecrow usually keeps them from stealing rice!"

"We're not Crows," the fourth Chough said. Another girl, she looked and sounded older than the others. But even she didn't supply an explanation for the straw man. Okamiko immediately discarded the question, realizing she didn't care why. If these children required no purpose to do what they did—and Okamiko knew, children often didn't—then she required no explanation.

Take was satisfied, too, but she heard him whispering excitedly and held him to her ear. Her eyes lit up and her tongue lolled out. "What an idea!"

"Thank you," the youngest chough-girl said. It was almost cheerful, with an air of finality, because she and her companions had gathered as many rice stalks as they could carry and were exiting the field.

"No, wait!" Okamiko cried, and caught up to them again. "I was thinking . . . or wondering . . . do you ever sell the things you make from straw?"

The Choughs stopped and performed their silent looking ritual again, each taking the other in, and then her.

"Why?" one of the boys asked finally.

Okamiko became embarrassed. She glanced sideways at Take, no longer certain she wanted to tell these children that the bamboo stick resting on her shoulder was her best friend. Even if the revelation didn't cause them to turn on her, to transform into cruel children who would throw rocks at her, it might ruin the deal she hoped to make.

"If weaving is your hobby," she said, "and your straw man is as amazing as your hats . . . I might like to have one."

"What do you have to trade?"

What *did* she have to trade? She had no idea. Aside from the rags she wore, her only possession was Take . . .

She leaned her ear toward him again. In unison, the Choughs cocked their heads to the left, either from confusion, or to mimic Okamiko and hear what she heard.

Okamiko listened for a moment. Then her eyes and mouth formed wide circles and she held Take at arm's length. "No! I can't!"

The Choughs straightened, then cocked their heads to the right this time, clearly from confusion. Okamiko continued to argue with the stick of bamboo.

"I won't!" she cried, and real tears pooled in her eyes.

"Won't what?" the other chough-boy asked.

She sniffed and glared at him, then shuddered, lowered her hairy head, and whispered, "Give you my stick."

"Then don't," the elder girl said. "It was your idea, not ours."

Three of the Choughs turned to leave. The fourth—the younger girl—stood clutching her bundle of rice and eyeing Take with curiosity. "What is it?" she asked finally.

"What do you mean, 'what is it'?" Okamiko growled. "Is *your* head stuffed with straw? It's bamboo!"

"We have bamboo," the eldest said, and again she made to lead the other three away. Again only the two boys moved to follow.

Undeterred, the youngest asked, "Is it *special* bamboo?"

The others paused.

Okamiko hugged Take against her wet cheek. "Of course it's special!" Then her eyebrows relaxed and she listened to the stick again. When the instructions only she could hear had ended, she started to protest. Then her shoulders drooped and her lower lip trembled.

"What did it say?" the youngest Chough asked in a voice halfway between suspicion and curiosity.

"Yes, it's special," Okamiko said to the ground, like a child made by a parent to recite formalities. "It is the Scepter of the Flying Geisha."

This time the chough-children did not perform their silent looking ritual, or cock their heads, or anything. They may have gripped their bundles of rice a little bit harder and leaned their curved red beaks a little bit closer, but they said nothing, perhaps expecting to be convinced. They waited on Okamiko, or the stick itself.

Okamiko dragged her gaze from the ground and peered at the Birds through her wild bangs, daring them to doubt her.

They did.

"You lie," one boy said.

"We have no time for games," the elder girl said.

"Where did you get it?" the other boy asked.

"Show us," said the youngest.

Okamiko replied with her own question: "How long will it take you to make the straw man?"

"One day," said the eldest.

"Then I will show you tomorrow. This time tomorrow. And if I can prove this is the Scepter of the Flying Geisha—"

"It's not," the boy said.

"—then we will trade. Okay?"

This time the silent looking ritual occurred without the youngest girl, who ignored her companions, hopped forward a pace to study Take more closely, then straightened and declared, "Okay" with a sweeping, scythe-like nod.

The elder girl yanked her back beside them, but didn't protest. Clearly curious herself, she simply said, "Not here."

The rice thieves obviously didn't want to be found at the scene of their crime. "Where?" Okamiko asked.

"At Tengu House."

"That's not in Oni. Where is it?"

The chough-girl pointed a red finger. "On that mountain, at the bridge over the river where the spider lilies grow."

Okamiko repeated this to herself a few times, until Take assured her he would remember. She nodded in agreement.

The chough-children said nothing more. Holding their bundles of rice close to their little bodies, they unfolded from their backs beautiful wings of black feathers. These were powerful enough to carry the children away through the sky, and flapping them created short gusts of air and ripples in the rice field. Okamiko might have enjoyed this and laughed happily, but she was distracted by worry, wondering how she was going to convince the Choughs that Take was really the weapon of the Flying Geisha, a mysterious, heroic legend no one had actually seen. He assured her he would take care of it, and so she wandered in search of something to eat and somewhere to spend the night.

⌇

The next day, Okamiko was waiting for the Choughs when they arrived. There was a peaceful pond and several streams and waterfalls spilling into it. The white blossoms from the overhanging trees were mirrored in the water, and some even drifted on its surface. All around were pink and red spider lilies; aptly named, their stems were tall and their pedals like spiders caught on their backs.

She stood at one end of a simple arch bridge which, to her fascination, was crafted from straw. Like the Choughs' conical rice hats, it was tightly woven, but thicker and heavier and capable of holding bodies that passed over it . . . especially light ones like the Choughs'.

They landed at the other end, on the side nearest the mountain and a three-story house high up its rocky slopes. Though it was still far away, Okamiko could see it, too, was built from straw, with large upward curving roofs in the traditional style. All this considered, she was even more eager to see what the Choughs had made for her.

The two boys bore it between them. When they flapped their wings around it, it held securely, not a straw blown out of place. The grains of rice had been harvested and the stalks bound together like strands of rope or chords of muscle, so that the yellow man-shape it made was, to Okamiko's delight, perfectly realistic and sturdy.

It was not a tall man, she noted, but the size one would expect four children to construct. It had knobby fingers and split-toe feet and, built onto the more complex patterns of its interwoven straw flesh, samurai armor running in parallel lines, including rectangular shoulder and thigh plates, bundled arm and shin guards, and a kabuto helmet. Inside this was the only item not made from straw: a grimacing mempo, or facemask, carved from bamboo. Like the Choughs themselves, this was red and had a long pointed nose.

This in particular won Okamiko over; this bamboo face was like Take personified, his identity recovered from the wood. She panted through a wide grin, as if witnessing the hard work that went into the straw man was exhausting in itself. "He's beautiful!" she said in awe.

Take agreed.

"Of course he is," the eldest chough-girl said. "That is why we require *three* demonstrations with your stick. Prove to us three times that it is the Scepter of the Flying Geisha and we will trade."

Okamiko wiped her nose, scratched her wild hair, and nodded. Taking a deep breath, she swept Take in front of her with both hands like a katana, her elbows pointing left and right. She waited.

The Choughs assumed she was pausing for instructions. The eldest prompted her. "They say the Flying Geisha can control the elements with her Scepter."

Okamiko nodded. She kept a straight face, waiting and trusting in Take. When nothing happened, her wide eyes briefly drifted to the side, and she smiled awkwardly. Through the side of her mouth she whispered, "What do I do?"

He told her to swing him in a circle, just as if he really was a sword. She obeyed immediately, stomping her foot forward and giving a proper *kiai* as she sliced the air.

To her surprise, the air responded.

A ripple of wind exploded from the bamboo's path, invisible and intangible until it reached the Choughs watching on the other end of the bridge. It blasted their feathers, filled their wings and carried them, all at once, a step backward from the straw man. They stood blinking, then performed that looking ritual of theirs.

Finally, the younger girl announced, "The first demonstration is acceptable."

The elder girl disagreed. "We can make wind, too," she said, and flapped her wings to return to her previous position in front of the straw samurai. Her companions joined her, and sure enough, Okamiko felt their wind blowing her hair. "Show us something better."

Okamiko was still looking at Take like she had never seen him before. Hearing the chough-girl, she wrung him in her dirty hands. Her fingernails were jagged, many of them broken or bitten off; she wondered if Take could manicure them. Would that be "something better"? She shook her shaggy head. Another weather demonstration, maybe? She examined the gray sky and the mist that drifted among the scraggly rocks and autumn trees, some green or blossoming white, most red and orange. Was Take powerful enough to reverse the fall, bring back summer? No, she thought.

Impatient, the eldest Chough prompted her again. "They say the Flying Geisha can make the tiniest of braids with her Scepter."

Okamiko thought about this, distracted for a moment by the question of what a chough-girl with feathers would need with a stick that makes braids. Then Take spoke up, telling her to touch him to her own wild bush of black hair. She obeyed.

She couldn't see what happened, of course, but like when the chough-children blasted her with their wings, she felt strokes brushing her hair, this time subtler and unceasing. She had never had her hair brushed before but it was pleasant and relaxing.

Slowly, one then two then three locks separated from the wild bush, controlled by invisible hands. The Choughs leaned their red beaks forward and peered with small dark eyes as the three locks began to intertwine. Okamiko's hair, though black, was not unlike straw, and she finally realized why such a technique might be interesting and useful to these expert straw weavers.

Before long, a single tight braid hung from a newly formed bun on the top of Okamiko's head, tied off with a supple leaf plucked from the rest of the tangled mess. The relaxing motions around her stopped, and she realized her eyes were closed. She opened them and held Take beneath a gaze of admiration.

She missed the Chough's looking ritual this time, if there was one, but heard the youngest girl announce, "The second demonstration is acceptable."

Again the elder girl disagreed. "That was no faster, but less effective, than our methods," she said with a hint of bitterness, and pointed a red finger at their straw samurai. "Show us something better!"

Something better? Okamiko couldn't imagine what that was. She looked the straw man up and down, agreeing that he was better, that he was perfect. She almost wished he was less so, that he was more like her in quality. She didn't deserve him, she realized, and let her head and stick droop in defeat.

There, on one end of the bridge, was Okamiko, alone. On the other, the Choughs. Between them, the straw samurai, who stood lifeless and unyielding.

Until it moved.

With a faint rustling, the statue of straw took one step forward. Then it took another. Then another. In this stilted soldier's march it approached Okamiko, but she didn't even notice until it was almost upon her. When she did, her eyes went wide and she leaned away as if to run, but her feet didn't budge.

The samurai lifted a straw arm and held out its straw hand, and Okamiko flinched, shutting her eyes. When nothing happened, she opened them again and saw the straw man was still, as if she had imagined the whole thing, as if someone—one of the children maybe—had waddled their statue across the bridge and positioned it here to frighten her. Its hand was still outstretched—and, she realized, open as if waiting to receive something. She raised her own hand, the one holding her bamboo stick, and began to wonder.

She leaned closer to the samurai's own bamboo face. "Take?"

The carved and painted grimace didn't move . . . and yet Okamiko reacted as if it did, as if the frown turned to a reassuring smile, the red cheeks and nose turning comical and friendly instead of violent and angry. Her own expression changed and she gave an animated shout.

"Take!"

On their end of the bridge, the Choughs' ritual played out more rapidly than usual.

Okamiko wanted to hug the straw samurai, but instead she obeyed its gesture and placed the bamboo stick—the old Take—into its open palm. Each intricately woven finger closed around it, and after a pause, the samurai performed a stiff about-face, holding the stick vertically before it with both hands. Like a sword. It began to march back the way it came.

The Chough children watched it come without moving or saying a word, their own bird-eyes wider than Okamiko's had been. The wait was simultaneously long and short: longer than a living man's march, shorter than one expects to wait on a straw man; long because none could wait to see what the living statue would do next, short because *any* action it made was too soon! It came on, until it finally stopped before the eldest chough-girl, who, it seemed to Okamiko, shrank a bit beneath its empty gaze.

This was where it would hand over the stick. It would make the exchange itself. Okamiko was thrilled and amazed. In spite of her own surprise, maybe even fear, the chough-girl held out her red hand in anticipation.

But the samurai didn't offer her the stick.

It hit her with it.

The action was swift—up above the kabuto helmet, then down, *whack*, and up again. The girl snatched back her stinging hand. Her feathered companions hopped a pace backward.

Okamiko laughed at first, thrilled at Take's prank. Then she saw the injured confusion in the girl's large eyes, and it was like looking in a mirror. She knew that feeling too well, and suddenly felt ashamed. She cried out Take's name.

He didn't listen to her. With the stick poised vertically beside his helmet, the samurai took a menacing step toward the Chough children. From behind the bamboo mask issued a deep, echoing chorus, like many voices speaking in unison.

They said, *Fly away.*

The children needed no more prompting than that. Their eldest, the girl who until now behaved like she was in charge, was the first to flee, nursing her hand while her wings pumped and feathers flew. The boys were quick to follow, and the fourth Chough, the younger girl, paused only a moment to give the straw samurai—*their* straw samurai—a final look of astonishment. It was theirs no more, and she, too, flapped away toward the straw house on the mountain slope.

"Wait!" Okamiko shouted after them, running past Take across the bridge. She watched the four black figures grow smaller and disappear. "You forgot the stick! I promised . . ."

She watched and waited long after it was clear the children weren't coming back. Part of her wished their parents would come swooping out of the house on larger wings, ready to discipline Okamiko like all the other parents in all the other villages. But none did. Still she waited, afraid to turn and face Take, who until now had never had a face.

"You really *are* the Scepter of the Flying Geisha," she said.

The straw samurai stood motionless, just as it had before, and for a brief moment Okamiko wondered if she had imagined it all. Then the stiff arms swung down like their joints gave way, and the bamboo stick clattered off the bridge into the water. Okamiko made a pained expression and a move to run after it, but the echoing voice stopped her.

No. It is just a lifeless stick. I created the wind. I braided your hair. I put on this straw man like clothes.

"You mean . . ." Okamiko started, hesitating out of embarrassment. "You mean, I didn't imagine you?"

No. I may not have a body, but that does not mean I am not real.

"That's why you wanted to trade!" she realized excitedly. "You're a spirit! You wanted a body!"

Yes.

But something new occurred to Okamiko. She thought back on her visits to the Dog village and all those unlucky accidents. Pots broken. Tools misplaced. Villagers knocked over.

"It was you," she whispered. "*You* pulled those pranks! You caused the bad luck, and *I* got blamed for it!"

Yes.

"But why?"

I did you a favor. All these villagers are Monsters. Do you really think you belong with them?

"No," she admitted, hanging her head. "Because I'm not like them. I'm not a Dog or a Cat or a Cow or a Chough. I'm human."

Yes. No fur or feathers or scales. No fangs or claws. Human. And humans can do anything.

Okamiko wiped her nose with a balled up little fist. "They can?"

Yes. And that is why we should trade.

"Trade? Trade what?"

Trade bodies.

Her nose and mouth twisted together. "Huh?"

You want to be different to fit in with those who are different. The Choughs would welcome back their living, walking, talking straw man.

"Who attacked them just now!"

Only in fun. You will make it right, and they will respect your power.

"Then come with me! We can return you together! Maybe they'll let me stay . . ."

No. You want to live among the Monsters. I wish to be human and live among humans. We have what each other wants. We need only trade.

"But how?" Okamiko laughed, throwing wide her arms. Were Take a child spirit, she wouldn't question him. But he was an adult spirit, which she hadn't realized until today. This was cause for caution.

Suddenly the air smelled heavier. The wind picked up, and with it came a different smell than the trees and blossoms and straw—the smell of metal. Okamiko looked around, now thinking she could see furtive figures moving on the upper bank of the pond. At first she blamed her imagination . . . but peering closer, she saw black feathers and the long, curved, red bill of an adult Chough, holding a long, curved sword in its red hand.

She knew she should be frightened; that she should run away, or scream, or give the straw samurai back to them.

Instead, she grinned and cheered, "Their parents didn't *fly* down! They sneaked!"

To punish you for tricking their children, Take said. *To drive you away like the others.*

Okamiko's grin faded. She looked at Take as if he had struck her. Before, he had always helped her maintain her illusions.

Trade bodies with me and you cannot be hurt, he said.

She considered his offer—not whether it was possible, which no longer bothered her, but whether it was right. Maybe she would be better off if she was like him. A straw samurai would not get cold at night. It would not drip blood or tears. It would not offend the villagers with its humanness.

"We would not hurt a child," someone said from behind Okamiko, interrupting her thoughts.

She turned to see one of the adult Choughs alight on the bridge. A male, he was virtually identical to the chough-children, but taller, fitter, and somehow more dignified. A parent, without doubt! He pointed a large iron war fan at Take, and other Choughs emerged on the bank bearing swords and poles.

"Our children told us what happened. We know the sound of a demon when we hear it. You have haunted this human!"

Are we not all "demons"? Take asked. His new straw body adopted a different stance, jerking as if the fit was not quite right, yet affecting man-like mannerisms that continued to disillusion and disappoint Okamiko: the shifting weight of his hips, his flexing fingers, the confident hand gestures . . . As a spirit he had spoken like a friend to her, betraying no selfish designs; now, with a body, he was all too transparent. *This human does not belong here*, he went on. *So I will take her and go.*

The chough-man flowed like water into a combat stance. "You will not."

Okamiko doubted what she was seeing. She was prone to misunderstandings and assumed that must be the case now. No one, least of all a Monster like this, would speak for her, let alone fight for her.

Thunder rolled in the sky, and no one paid it any heed. Then it continued, growing louder. It didn't come from the sky, they realized, but from the trees down the mountain, in the direction of Oni. Everyone turned and waited until a small herd of Cows and Pigs spilled out of the forest, big and fat and running on two legs, their hooves kicking up dust. Okamiko recognized their farmers' weapons waving in the air—rakes and flails and sickles and clubs.

Their Pig leader paused when he saw the straw man, the straw bridge, and the straw house, then pointed and squealed a command. The herd came charging forward. The pond rippled and the bridge shook. For a moment Okamiko thought the heavy beasts might storm it, an image that struck her as comical; but they stopped along the bank opposite the Choughs and glared at them, snorting angrily. Their huge bodies and curved horns were intimidating, yet they seemed uneasy in sight of the tall, unmoving Bird warriors. Okamiko realized that she had never seen two different villages interact.

The Pig leader, simple-looking and weary, pointed a pink finger at the Chough near her on the bridge. "So it is you," he said in an old, phlegmatic voice. "Stealing our rice. All this proves it!"

"We tend our own terraced paddies here in the mountains," the Chough leader replied calmly, and left it at that. Okamiko wondered if he didn't know what the children had done, or intentionally guarded their secret. She liked to believe it was the latter.

The cow- and pig-people murmured and their leader shook his leafy ears. "Lies. A trail leads here from a fresh-cut field. Our field."

"That settles it, then," the Chough said, and stretched his wings like a peacock. "Our kind leave no trails."

The herd counseled together angrily. Okamiko felt their attention turn to her and tried to smile, hoping they would recognize her, but realized that was likely to make matters worse.

"The human, then," the Pig declared finally. "You've made her this playmate from our stolen straw. Give us the rice you harvested and we'll go."

"The playmate is all that is left."

This caused new murmuring. Perhaps from a desperate need for justice, the Pig cried out, "Then return *it* to us!"

Though Take had, perhaps, betrayed her, Okamiko's concern for him was automatic. On the other hand, both he and the Choughs *had* stolen the straw, and the Oni villagers certainly deserved compensation.

But the Chough leader surprised her again. Take was not his priority.

"Have it," he said, "but do not trust it. There is a demon in that straw who seeks to possess this girl. No doubt it will inspire other humans against us, the same as all our ancestors."

This time when the herd murmured, it was without anger, in low, curious, patient whispers. The essence of those whispers was the same question: Were demons to blame for their quarrel with humans?

Enough, Take said. He turned his straw body toward Okamiko, confirming to everyone he was alive, but ignoring their gasps and grunts. *We are teammates. Remember? And the teams are uneven again. Tell them* you *chose* me. *Tell them we belong together. Tell them, and we can go.*

She felt everyone's eyes on her. Attention she was used to, but for it to be quiet, considerate, even eager, was an unfamiliar sensation. It was uncomfortable and empowering all at once.

There was weight in those eyes. The reflection they returned this time was not plain and unremarkable, but, for reasons she still didn't understand, important. But none were as heavy as the ones without a reflection; those carved into the straw samurai's bamboo mask; those hiding invisible behind it.

"Take . . ." she said, hoping to call an end to this game.

Choose, Okamiko!

She stared at her feet, wishing, for once, that she was alone.

I did not abandon you to these Monsters, Take whispered, like he was that soundless, innocent voice in her ear again. *Do not abandon me.*

She looked up. "But you tried to."

The red mask looming over her withdrew somewhat, that pointy nose suddenly less accusing.

"You tried to," Okamiko repeated, gaining confidence. "You said you wanted to trade bodies. You said you wanted to leave me here."

Okamiko . . .

"I think you were using me all along," she continued. "I think you were never my friend."

The Chough warriors began to inch forward, even as the straw samurai took a step back.

And suddenly, the decision was easy.

"Goodbye, Take," she said.

He snarled, and grabbed her through her wild bush of hair. His straw fingers gripped her skull tightly, their joints crackling. Suddenly she felt very strange . . . like she was about to vomit through all of her pores.

If you love them instead of me, be *them instead of me!*

Then he dropped her, and through a flurry of black feathers she saw why. He was under attack.

She was horrified to realize he could move quickly, and, though weaponless, was holding his own, turning blades aside with flat palms, chopping and kicking until a disarmed katana found its way into his hands. Metal rang fiercely, but Okamiko missed most of it, because a different battle boiled inside her. She was doubled over, twisting and groaning as her little body began to transform.

What she missed, as her hairiness spread, was Take defeating the Chough warriors.

What she missed, as her nails and teeth grew longer, was the Chough leader blowing Take to the bank with his war fan.

What she missed, as her legs twisted, was the Oni villagers taking up the fight.

What she missed, as her nose and ears grew out, was Take using their own strength against them.

What she missed, as she lay panting in pain, was a beautiful figure descending from the sky.

Her face felt soft against the straw bridge. The mountain rocks and the Tengu House were stacked sideways, and the sky was in the wrong place. A woman was speaking somewhere behind her. She couldn't see her, but heard every word:

"Afraid to speak now that I'm here? Afraid I might recognize you? Are you one or many? Never mind. I've heard in the West they cast demons like you into beasts. If it's a body you crave, why not that Pig?"

Nervous oinking brought the face of the Pig leader to mind.

"No," the woman continued, "I forgot. You only *make* Monsters. Who, then, is the real monster, I wonder? Can we tell by the outside . . . or the in?"

Something happened then, something Okamiko only sensed. She knew it was amazing and mighty and moving, yet the only sound she heard was the crash of leaves. No, not leaves; straw.

"There," the woman said. "You have mimicked the Scepter's power well, but you can never match it. Even you feel its scars. I suggest you return from where you came before it gives you more."

A breeze blew by that wasn't a breeze. It retrieved something from Okamiko, a light trace that escaped in a gasp. Then it was gone.

Take was gone.

As Okamiko struggled to rise, she saw a snow white hand reach down to her. The hand that took it—her own—was soft and covered in fur. The woman helped her to her feet (feet that were paws) and Okamiko saw the large black-and-white wings first, then the smooth, smiling face of the Flying Geisha.

"You're a Butterfly," Okamiko said, because it was true.

"And you are a Wolf child," the Flying Geisha said. She smoothed Okamiko's fur and pointed down at the pond.

Hesitant at first, Okamiko finally peeked over the bridge's rail at her reflection in the water. She was surprised at what she saw:

Herself.

BLACK BIRDS

Laura Blackwood

Lisa woke to a crow perched on her dresser. She tried to ignore it, though she knew it wouldn't ignore her. It flew to the bathroom, the rustle of its feathers like silk being rubbed together, and preened itself on the towel rack as she showered and got ready for work.

It spoke as she was putting on her makeup. "Your face can't distract from those sixty extra pounds. That GoodLife membership was money well spent, huh?" Nothing she hadn't thought to herself now and then. No need to answer. She had too much work to do today to get distracted.

On the drive in, she played catchy pop songs and sang along while the crow clicked its beak and grumbled. It hopped about her desk as she worked, bright black eyes missing nothing.

When she emailed the wrong version of a press release to the proofers, it spoke. "Wow. Only four months in and you're getting sloppy. Maybe this job should've gone to someone who can actually pay attention?"

Lisa attached the right document and joked about Mondays in her follow-up email. She closed her eyes, inhaling deeply. Time for some positive self-talk: it was just a slip up. Anybody could make it.

"Lisa?"

Her eyes snapped open. Katja stood at her office door, holding a time-off request form. Heat stung Lisa's cheeks at the thought of what she must have looked like sitting at her desk, eyes closed, desperate for calm and the day not even begun yet.

As Lisa joked about needing more coffee and asked how Katja's weekend was, the crow tsked. Its "Way to look professional!" was just a little bit louder than Katja's answer.

∼

Winter collapsed on Edmonton the second week of October, and a magpie joined the crow. It was beautiful: a tail long as her forearm, black feathers interrupted by shocking white or shifting to bottle-green depending on the light. They both watched her cut into her filet mignon during her bimonthly night out with the girls, listening.

When Lisa started spacing out as Katy and Vanessa enthused about their favourite TED Talks, the crow muttered, "Bored of your best friends already?" The crow liked questions and never expected answers.

The magpie screamed, "Bitch!"

Lisa had to get out of her own head; she made herself pay attention. She talked about her new job, told some funny stories about her co-workers, asked about Sarah's wedding plans and asked Vanessa how her volunteering was going.

"Really?" The crow cocked its head at her. "Surface-level conversation with people you've known all your life? Ash was right—you're so closed off. There's just nothing below the chit-chat, is there?"

As if a fun night out with friends demanded so much depth.

Katy looked up from her phone. "Lis, you haven't unfriended that bitch? She dumped you months ago."

The response, by now, was automatic: their lives had been going in different directions, but she and Ash had agreed to be friends.

Vanessa switched topics quickly.

"She's embarrassed by you," the crow said. "They all are. You can't even break up with someone right."

"Useless fucking cunt!" the magpie shouted. It walked across her plate with the stilted, jerky strut of a wind-up toy soldier and left a white, sticky puddle on her steak. Her throat closed up. She forced herself to eat another piece. It took two sips of wine to wash it down.

Later that evening, as Lisa was driving Katy back to her place, Katy asked if she was okay. "You seemed kinda distant tonight."

Unbidden, Lisa's darkest time at the U of A flashed through her mind: sobbing over her stats textbook, beyond words, facing the collapse of the psych degree she'd worked her entire first year for. Katy had stroked her back, murmured soothingly, made tea. After the third hour, Katy had suggested she see someone. The exact words had faded, but Lisa still remembered the crackle of impatience Katy would later deny. Lisa had known what she meant: see someone *else*. Someone who can deal with how fucked up you are. And Lisa had tried—shrink after shrink, pill after pill, for years, until some obscure magic had come together and the world opened up again.

Lisa told Katy she was a bit stressed from the new job. She meant the crow and magpie to hear it, too. This wasn't like university. This wasn't like before. She just needed to sleep better, eat healthier.

"You ever need a spa day, I've got a Groupon," Katy said. "I'll hook you up, girl."

Lisa murmured her thanks.

The crow scoffed.

Wings whirred as she got ready for her date; she glanced from her reflection to see a gray jay fluttering past the bathroom door. Compared to the crow and the magpie, it looked teddy-bear sweet, with gleaming black eyes in its white face.

It hovered by her window and pointed outside with its beak, where snow fell heavily. "You don't want to drive in this weather, do you? There were two accidents on the Henday yesterday." During the car ride, Lisa discovered the jay never landed, but flew tirelessly in circles.

She got to DaDeO fifteen minutes early.

"Desperate fat dyke!" hooted the magpie as she waited, sipping water and playing Bejeweled.

"Maybe you should leave and come back at two?" said the jay. "You don't want to look needy."

"Thirty-five years old and back in the dating game," said the crow. "There's no way you can't look needy, there."

The jay's fluttering increased as two o'clock came and went and Lisa's phone didn't buzz.

"The servers are starting to stare," the jay said. "They might kick you out for not ordering."

After half an hour, Lisa texted Marly and asked where she was.

"You might have waited too long," said the jay. "She probably thinks you don't care."

"!" Marly texted back. "shit sorry, thot i txted u, mace's sick puke everywhere! rain check? thurs?"

Lisa hoped Mason got well soon and said her Thursday was free. Sorrow tightened in her chest. She felt like she'd failed a test, somehow. Tears blurred her vision. She pretended to examine the menu to hide her face.

"Stop crying, you fucking bitch!" shouted the magpie.

This was nothing. She'd make it nothing. Lisa practised her Sama Vritti—inhale for four counts, exhale for four through the nose. This was just dirt muddying the water of her mind. Let it sink to the bottom.

The magpie preened itself, the crow flapped behind her, and the jay kept fluttering but said nothing. She flagged a server down and ordered oysters. As she did, talons rested on her shoulder, hot as brands. The crow spoke quietly into her ear.

"If this goes any further than a first date, there'll be a kid." It chuckled, feathers ruffling. "C'mon—you as a mom? You're way too selfish for that."

It weighed far more than any bird should.

೦ೞ

At the senior management meeting, Lisa knocked over her coffee cup. It fell in slow motion. She saw the first droplets spatter her notes, then the lake of the spill spread across the table and trickle down onto her new skirt—her Christmas present to herself. Cream-coloured, of course. Silk.

The magpie shouted "Shit!" in her voice. Out loud. In front of the president and CEO of the company. They looked at her as if seeing her for the first time, then at each other. She knew what that meant.

"They think you can't handle things," the jay said, swooping low over the president's head. "That you're cracking under the pressure."

A few people winced and one or two chuckled as she apologized, grabbed some napkins near the platter of muffins and wiped it up, then left for the washroom to clean her skirt. The crow adjusted its weight as she moved—these days, it only flew to flap from one shoulder to the other.

The stain sat on her skirt like a scar for the rest of the day.

That evening, out for drinks with Katy, she told the story. She meant it to come out with a sigh and an eye roll, but the gray jay started speaking in her voice. "It was so embarrassing! I can't believe I did that. I just stood there gaping like an idiot . . ."

It talked until Katy rolled her eyes and said, "Jesus, enough about the coffee!"

Fear cracked through her and Lisa made herself grin and turn the conversation to when Josh was going to propose, which got Katy on a good long rant.

Later that night, the crow made a good point. "No one sees what they don't want to. No one will see us unless you give us away."

Something like satisfaction warmed her. At least she had that.

೦ೞ

Lisa clicked through her friends' Facebook profiles. Sarah had just uploaded the photo album from her wedding in Mexico. Every time Lisa saw herself in those photos, she frowned. The entire vacation felt like a foggy, half-remembered dream. She wished she'd had as much fun as it looked like she was having. The crow was right; what kind of person couldn't enjoy an all-inclusive resort?

She clicked through Pinterest and took some Buzzfeed quizzes. She had a second browser tab open, but she didn't look at it. That was her credit card bill, and she didn't need to think about that right now. The gray jay had whimpered when it saw the number and was now dashing frantically about the room. The magpie was still swearing, but she'd grown so used to that over the past few months that she could make it into background noise.

She noticed when the birds went silent. The crow flew from her shoulder, replaced by something heavier: a raven. It was monstrously big compared to the birds she saw every day. The other birds watched the raven respectfully, courtiers on the arrival of their ruler—the jay even perched.

"It's tiring, isn't it?" the raven asked kindly. It reminded her of a friendly youth pastor. "Is this really what you want? Days and days of . . . this?" It gestured to her living room with its thick beak, gray as iron. Empty. Instinctively, she looked around for Lady, only to remember that she was in an urn on the bookshelf. Not even a cat anymore.

She thought about trying her breathing exercises, but didn't. She reached for the mindfulness she'd once had.

The crow perched on her other shoulder, interrupting her. "The job, the money . . . you know it doesn't mean anything. You don't have anyone to share it with, anything to pass on."

Her gaze went to Lady's urn. Someone had loved her, once. Needed her.

"A person should think of friends and family, first," the crow said. "Not an animal."

She glanced at her tablet, remembering Sarah's beautiful ceremony.

"They wouldn't be your friends if they knew what you were," the crow continued.

The magpie hopped by her feet. "A fucking selfish whore," it grumbled, its usual rage dampened.

The crow shuffled closer to her ear. "Lis . . . you feel like shit when your life is going good."

The gray jay started flying again. "Something bad is going to happen. The pipes will break. You'll get attacked. Get into a car accident. Your mom's getting older—you'll have to put her into a home."

"What'll happen when the shit hits the fan?"

She'd been happy, once. Hadn't she?

"You couldn't help being this fucked up. An only child. A single mother who spoiled you rotten. You never got what people need."

She'd loved swimming at the cabin at Pigeon Lake. Once, she'd spent an entire afternoon following a school of minnows—not to catch them, just to follow and be a part of them, move how they moved, swim where they swam. They'd shimmered in the sunlight like buried treasure.

"That's it?" The crow sighed. "Your happiest memory is a lake? You do realize that even in your happiest memory, you're still alone, right? All you've got are these pathetic little scraps of a life . . ."

She almost went to Ash's Facebook page, but stopped herself. All she could remember of Ash was the pain. She tried to think of Mom, but could only remember the desperate undertone of 'grandchild' that always came up in any conversation with her. There'd been no heartache or expectations with those fish, with a cat so dumb she couldn't figure out how to leave a room when the door was only open a crack.

There was a flicker of movement above Lady's urn. The shimmer of fish filling in the outline of a cat. The scarecrow had Lady's bright yellow eyes. Lisa braced herself for platitudes, for condescension, for fakeness. The scarecrow opened its mouth.

The raven spoke over it, as if patiently explaining something to a small child. "It took years before you found the right drugs. Years before you found someone to listen. Do you want more years of that?"

"Get some sleep," the scarecrow said. "The questions will still be there tomorrow. Sleep's not too difficult, right? You're so tired lately."

The raven stared at the scarecrow, beak thrust forward like a dagger. The scarecrow stared back.

The scarecrow was right. Sleep, she could do. As Lisa got ready for bed, she stroked the raven's feathers. They were startlingly, achingly soft. Then the scarecrow leaped onto her bed, like Lady used to, and curled on her chest.

"See you in the morning," the scarecrow said.

Wings rustled in the dark. Beaks clicked. One of the birds cawed. But none of them spoke.

EDITH AND I

Virginia Carraway Stark

The cool autumn mist that coated the branches of the birch trees and the stubble of hay left in the dying fields reminded me of memories I couldn't possibly have. I had been born in the late spring, after the fields had melted and the garden planted. I had never seen fall before and yet it coursed through my essence. Even though my purpose had been to stand in the fields and guard the tiny blazes of life that germinated there from greedy beaks, my strength only started to come to me as the nights grew chill and the leaves fell. Before, I was a sleepy observer, watching the world through the caul of half-closed eyes.

I had a dreamy awareness after Edith's strong fingers and thick sewing needle made me out of a pair of old coveralls and her dead husband's snap up plaid shirt taken from the rag box.

She stuffed me with hay until I stood rigid and then my arms stood out at awkward angles no living person would hold themselves and formed my head from a burlap sack.

She embroidered a mouth on me. Large and smiling, with the edges of teeth showing, then pulled the burlap so my lips puckered and my face stretched beyond the two dimensions that would leave me only a paper doll. That was the important part, that my head be the right shape to convince the birds the garden wasn't worth the risk of braving me, to convince the canny living that I too was alive and a threat. She added large glass beads in sun-catching blue for my eyes so they would sparkle like I was alive.

That's when I first saw her broad, careworn face.

She had the thread in her mouth, smoothing the frayed ends to rethread the needle so she could sew my eyelashes She added a black curly wig from last Halloween to my head and sewed it and the floppy fisherman's hat in place. She looked at me critically, added some hay to thicken my neck and jammed my abruptly ending legs into large rubber boots.

This was the start of me. My birth. I didn't feel pain then—I rustled with newly-settling hay as she jammed the post up the back of my shirt and now surveilled the kingdom my goddess had given to me.

It was muddy and lay in dark furrows of barren readiness. Magpies and crows at the far end of the garden hunted for worms and beetles in the freshly-plowed ground and watched us . . . sizing me up, appraising me. I knew even then, in my dream of life, that I had to be threatening as well as lively. I had to emote danger and be ever ready to pounce without the power of movement. Edith needed me and I couldn't fail her. Serving her was my sole purpose in life.

The seasons passed and I was successful in my menacing.

It wasn't easy.

I pulled up energy from the warming soil and radiated menace. I drew up a shudder if the crows came near, the trembling, convincing earth energy of the living. I thanked my creator for my features that captured the sunlight and the wind that rustled my hair and wobbled me about on my anchored spine. The seeds had the time they needed and germinated.

I watched them come up out of the ground, little coy green pokes and spirals. I smiled at them with my teeth and guarded their fragrant beauty with new energy. These were my children with my Lady. They were a part of her, a part of me, and a part of the sun and rain that landed on us all. They had to be guarded for what was to come, for the shortening of days and the fullness of their harvest.

I stood with her while she tended them. She talked to me and I listened to the rise and fall of her words without a need for comprehension. She sang songs her mother had sung and recited poetry with playful formality. She stood like a schoolgirl with her hands folded on the handle of spade as she orated to me and the new plants. Sometimes, with sparkling, laughing malice she would say the poems at the birds who watched her from a safe distance. Her voice would rise and the birds' voice would follow in angry response at her daring to confront them with the magic words her father had taught her.

She would sing, her voice low, roughened with age, while squishing the pests that plagued the garden. These were dangers my eyes could not see and I had only my faith in my goddess that she would bring the young plantlings through yet another danger.

Eventually, they plumped up with flowers and fruits. Soon I was hidden up to my waist, then vines climbed my shoulders and twined around my face. Flowers bloomed like trumpets on me and then came the bees and then the fruits. First small, then large and larger still. Before long I was burdened with their heaviness, but my spine was strong and it didn't trouble me. I slept through the hot, sun-filled days, buried in the life I had helped nurture.

It was the chill in the air that woke me once more. Night time chill that left me and the children of the garden covered in heavy, wet dew. The moon was high and full and Edith was standing before me in the fey light. She smiled when she saw I was awake and lifted a glass of wine high to the moon above us. Her feet were bare and her dress hung down to her knees in tatters. Her sun-browned face was wrinkled and her eyes were those of a young girl. She drank the wine, spilled some on my galoshes and drank the rest lifting her voice in triumphant song. Then she turned and walked away but I could hear her song even after the door to the house closed and the flicker of candles beckoned to me from her window.

I had slept too long, my feet were rooted to the ground and the crops depended on me. I fell asleep under the moon with the vision of Edith pouring wine on my feet filling my mind.

I watched her on her knees in front of me as she rooted up the carrots. She worked with her head down, humming and talking as she tested and uprooted the orange miracles. Soon it was the corn and then the gourds, one by one the fruits of our labours were brought in. She walked by me on the path, pushing the wheelbarrow in front of her, and later I could hear her in her kitchen preparing the vegetables for winter storage.

I came awake to the landscape. I could see clearly now, beyond the gently sloping garden, past the thin line of trees to the hay field beyond. Nothing was growing anymore. The nights were too cold and the autumn sun too thin and weak to push plants out of the ground.

That was the first reaping and another soon followed. With the garden harvested, Edith drove the pigs into the garden. They rooted through the soil and tugged the vines off of my shoulders. They ate everything in their path and tromped the fertilizer they left behind into the soil. The weeds were sought out and mercilessly destroyed along with the ruins of the year that was now dying. Next year's harvest would be a rich one.

And still, my energy surged upward. The pigs rutted, mated and fought over the last snippets of green the soil harboured.

Edith watched them and fed them her scraps. She no longer had the eyes of a young mother. She had aged along with the year and she watched the pigs with the same canny appraisal that the magpies and crows had watched us plant our seeds that spring. She was the crone now and barren. We must prepare for the maiden of spring together, we must make the path rich and clear for her young, bare feet when she awoke in the growing light of spring.

The next day she brought the kitchen knife with her. It was long and sharp. The blade curved inward from being repeatedly being sharpened year after year. It was the same one she had cut the gourd's free from their vines with.

She drove the pigs one by one into a wire cage and plunged the knife into their throats. Their screams echoed throughout the rolling hills and they panicked as she sought out the ones she had marked in her mind for slaughter. Her criteria was invisible to me, perhaps it was invisible to the pigs as well, or maybe not. They didn't talk to me so I don't know.

Their blood soaked into the field. This was needed, it had always been needed. Life sprung from blood. The blood of the mother on her birthing bed, the blood of the sacrifice in the field.

The land hummed. It was bare on the surface, the leaves had all fallen to the ground, but to me, it felt more alive than ever before.

That night, snowflakes fell and the little pools of blood turned them red and then pink and then a thin blanket of white covered the garden and me.

I ripped free of my moorings and, with my heavy rainboot feet shuffled across the snow. The snow under my feet sounded crisp. I had shed my spine behind me and my head lay against my right shoulder.

I leaned against Edith's windowpane, crushing the brim of my hat. She must have gone to bed but she'd left a candle to burn in a brass bowl in each of the windows.

With my slow, shuffling pace I made my way to the front porch. I rested on the forced-willow bench with my head against the frame of the door. I would rest awhile longer, I would see if the moon penetrated the clouds and if the stars shone against the snow.

I would pick my time and I would knock on Edith's door.

I would knock and see if she answered and if maiden's blood still stirred her in the dark, secret places or if she slept now the sleep of the crone.

I thought of the look of promise in her eyes as she spilled wine at my feet and thought I heard the creak of slow footsteps on the wooden floor inside.

SCARECROW PROGRESSIONS (RUBBER DUCK REMIX)

Sara Puls

I once knew a girl who feared she'd transform into a scarecrow overnight. To prevent this nightmare from spawning into a thing of reality against her will, she undertook to become one of her own accord. She began with the obligatory hat-of-straw, sewing it into her scalp as quick and sure-fingered as her grandmother fastened renegade buttons back into place on her grandfather's dress shirts. That is how she described it anyway; we did not meet until some time after the hat took up permanent residence in the taut flesh of her head. The hat, aside from being the first step down the path of no return, was a touch green in hue and complimented her strawberry-blonde hair as well as anything could. For thread, she selected a thick, sturdy number the color of ghosts and dread. She showed it to me once, because I begged, and I puked on my shoes.

I first saw her at the carnival one night late in June. I was twenty-two, in love with mandarin oranges, and in denial about my penchant for self-inflicted pain. My fingernails were full of dirt, as was my t-shirt, and a bit of metal, or possibly a dead goldfish, had found its way into my boots. I'd worked as a carnie several years, but had just been transferred from "ride jock" to "duck pond operator." I considered this a demotion, a low among lows, so during lulls, and also when we were busy, I freed my brain from my head and let it wander. I spent my breaks behind the bunkhouse, smoking cigarettes and eating mandarin oranges, and she would meet me there, wearing clothes that were too big and lipstick that was too red. Sometimes she'd come close enough to take an orange slice or bum a cigarette, and our fingers would brush together. Feathers in the breeze.

"What would you want to be instead?" I asked her once. "I mean, if you weren't obsessed with becoming a scarecrow?"

"I'm not *obsessed*," she said, "I'm just accepting my fate in advance."

"Have you ever met a human who has turned into a not-human?"

She shook her head. "But I couldn't become anything else, even if I tried." She spoke with something of a lisp, but not quite. It was like lemonade in August.

I took a drag on my cigarette and stepped closer but she stepped away. I could hear people screwing in the bunkhouse. Ramon and Lisa, if I had to guess. Most of the things you hear about carnies are made up, but that one is true: they really do like to screw. I wondered if she heard them too, but was afraid I'd blush if I put the thought into words. So instead I muttered, "That sounds like nonsense."

Frowning, she tugged at her hat and winced. "Maybe it's fatalistic, but it isn't nonsense."

I didn't ask what fatalistic meant, in part because it would have conflicted with my attempts to view myself as smarter and saner than this girl who had sewn a hat into her scalp. Also because I just wanted to sit and look at her without worrying about the meaning of things. I wanted to forget about where we were, about how doubtful it was we'd ever share a kiss, about all the things that can go wrong in a life.

Later, a toddler barfed in the duck pond.

Some dude kicked off his shoes on the Gravitron and one of them hit an old lady in the head.

A kid swallowed a live goldfish. His mother threatened to have me fired.

Once, I found her behind the bunkhouse just after sunup. Half the sky was still that orangey-pink of push-up pops, the other half the pale blue of a robin's egg. She was humming the melody to a song I didn't know, but struck me faintly as something from The Wizard of Oz. Her voice made my bones feel mushy, and warm.

The first thing she said to me that morning was, "You could get killed working here, you know?"

I laughed, and she pretended to smile.

She wasn't all that attractive, but then neither was I. And what did it matter, anyway? I liked the way her mouth moved when she spoke. I liked her fingers, which were long and skinny, and I liked her fingernails, which she painted a purplish black (I assumed to invoke suggestions of blue corn). And even though I thought she was crazy, or at least half-so, I was envious of her ability to commit to a project and really see it through. I was full of ideas, hundreds of bright and shiny ideas, but I spent my time watching grimy plastic ducks swim round and round a grimy plastic pool.

"I'm serious," she said, taking one tiny step towards me. "You could die here."

By then she wore only men's plaid shirts, which she purchased from thrift shops and garage sales. She also smelled faintly of hay, which was the newest development in her scarecrow progressions. I was under the impression most perfumes were made with scents like flowers or fruits, or on rare occasion, what I considered to be some of the less disgusting herbs. But still, I let myself think it was just perfume, not some ominous change in the constitution of her innards.

It's amazing: the things we tell ourselves to keep from going crazy, or to be certain that we do. The things we do because we're too scared to do different, better things.

"The Ferris wheel could fall on your head," she continued. "You could get food poisoning from spoiled funnel cake batter. Those little ducks could turn into crows or magpies or blue jays and peck you to death."

"I doubt any of those things will happen. The last one never will."

"You're wrong," she whispered, now stern and serious. "That one's more likely than the rest."

"Oh really?" I snarked. I wanted her to know that even though I liked her I *knew* she was a loon. I also wanted her to know I wasn't a fool. (Actually I was, but I spent a lot of effort trying to prove that I wasn't.)

"Yes," she said, wiping her forehead. It was at least a hundred degrees outside, and humid too. Her eyes were glossy and wet, like marbles fresh out of a child's mouth. I wondered: had they always been that dark and round? Even now, I'm not sure.

I leaned back against the bunkhouse (it was a pale reddish color that, in certain lights, matched her hair). Then, because I couldn't look at her, I took a drag on my cigarette and dug one heel into the dirt as if it were the most important task in the world.

"It wouldn't be your fault," she added. "Or the fault of this carnival. Or the result of too many bodily fluids contaminating the duck pond. It'd be mine."

I wanted to tell her she was full of shit. But I could tell she believed it, and because of that so did I. So we stood there in silence, both fidgeting and not looking at each other. Both with too many sad thoughts sloshing in our heads.

After a while, she sat down in the grass, which was mostly just dirt and cigarette butts and bits of trash.

I sat next to her, and pulled an orange from my pocket. "Here," I said, holding it out over her lap.

Her nose wrinkled. "No thanks."

I pulled the orange back towards me and started peeling it. "What, scarecrows don't eat oranges?"

"Scarecrows don't eat."

This made me sad, like the time I tore a hole in the crotch of my favorite jeans, only sadder. I wanted to stand up, and run in circles, and shout: fuck your stupid game, fuck the feigned insanity, fuck sadness. Just fuck all of it. We're already dying, day by day, let's not hurry it along.

But I couldn't. It wasn't just that. What I really wanted to say was—was that she was kind and smart and I . . .

I just couldn't get my brain to be as bold as my heart.

In my hesitation, she scooted away from me, then glared at me out of the corner of her eye. "Don't pretend you know anything about being me. You don't know real problems. You can just pack up and leave."

I could, in theory. Except my carnival was not the kind that moved to a new city every few days. The owners were growing old, and tired, and so we put down roots for weeks at a time, sometimes longer. You might think regular folks would fast become bored with Ferris wheels and cotton candy and colored lights. But they don't. Any decent-sized city has enough children and stoners and couples on first dates, and most of all sad, middle-aged men angling for a piece of ass, to facilitate the modest lifestyle of a few dozen carnies for a considerable while.

So there I was, in that town way down at the border of Texas and Mexico, where everyone who was anyone spoke both Spanish and English, where lime trees and stray dogs were as common as barbacoa and hundred-degree days.

"I'm not going anywhere," I said.

But even then I knew: nothing lasts forever. I knew it was too damn easy to say words you couldn't mean for long. Either I would leave, or she would grow tired of me and stop coming around. Either I would die—of funnel-cake poisoning or a heart attack or a freak duck pond accident—or she would succumb to her fear-filled aspirations before I had the chance.

"Well *I* am," she said. "So I guess it doesn't matter anyway."

"Yeah. I guess."

I married her once, or at least I wish I had. It happened on a Sunday night, after everyone had left, after my fellow carnies had gone out to drink or off to sleep. Despite the heat, she had on a pink-and-blue flannel shirt. It had faded almost to white on one shoulder, and both of the elbows were threadbare, and one button had lost its way.

But to me, she looked pretty, even if too thin, and much *much* too tired.

"Wanna ride the Ferris wheel?" I asked, because in all that time, I'd never once seen her get on a ride. "Or are you scared?"

She pushed my shoulder with two fingers, which zapped a thrilling tightness into my chest. "I'm not *scared*. I'm not scared of anything."

She was lying, of course, but I didn't mind. "C'mon then. Let's go." I took her by the hand (she didn't shy away from me this time) and led the way.

The moon was out, and nearly full, so the pastel seats looked bright and inviting against the sky. I helped her into a seat, got the machine going, and jumped in beside her with the grace and cunning and agility that only ride jocks—or former ones, in my case—have. When I looked at her, she was smiling a little, in this far off, desperate way. I think about that smile still, when I'm alone, most of all when I'm fighting to stuff my head with other things. At the ride's highest point, I took a plastic ring from my pocket, which I found floating in the duck pond earlier that day, and handed it to her.

"Like a real carnie wedding," I joked, except wishing it were anything but a joke. "That's how most carnies get married, right here at the top of the wheel."

She didn't say anything, but she took it from me, and slipped it onto her ring finger, and closed her eyes.

Right then, into that almost peaceful silence, I should have said, 'Let's always be good to each other. I know that isn't something you can really promise, I know bits of people fall away and change, and new, strange bits grow up, making us all monsters and beasts, but let's try? Okay?' Because that would have been a real thing to say. That would have been true. And maybe she'd have realized, then, that a part of me understood what she was, what she was doing, what she wanted to undo.

But instead, I kept quiet until our feet were on the ground again, where I blurted out, "I think I love you." It was the most childish thing you could say to someone you barely knew and I hated myself for it before the curve of the words faded from my tongue.

"I know," she said, looking sadder than ever, "but every love story is also a horror story."

I didn't know what that meant, then, or what to make of it, but it hit me like a punch in the gut all the same. After that, I didn't see her for a while.

A kid broke his leg jumping off the carousel. A little girl gave me a dandelion and said it was because my eyes looked too sad. Another kid kicked me in the knee because he didn't like his prize.

When my girl finally showed up again, she wasn't wearing the plastic ring. I offered her my cigarette as if I hadn't noticed, as if everything were normal, fine. It was too late to ask how she was, or if she needed help, or if she knew how much I needed her.

She declined the cigarette, making a *poof* motion with her hands. "I could go up in flames."

Tired of playing along, or maybe too sad to try, I just shrugged.

She didn't seem to notice my exasperation, and got right to the point of her visit. "I need your help. Today is the day. Beneath my skin, I'm going to turn into straw or timothy or maybe even alfalfa. And that's it. That's the last thing there is. I picked a field not far from here, and I put a post in the ground. It's waiting for me."

"And?" I asked. "What on earth do you need me for?"

"I don't want to make you do it, but I don't have anyone else."

I could have guessed what she wanted, part of me already knew, but I thought maybe if she couldn't say it either, then it wouldn't come true.

She paused, and pulled a length of rope from her purse. "I need you to prop me up and secure me, okay?" She was looking at me, but also not at all. It was more like she was looking at the whole deep, dark universe. Straight on.

That was her problem. Or one of them. Nobody, I don't think, is strong or sane enough to look at the world like that. My problem, of course, was that I refused to take a peek, a chance, any risk at all.

I opened my mouth but she cut me off.

"—No. It's happening. You know it and so do I."

"But why?" I asked, fighting to ignore the burn in my eyes. "Why are you doing this?"

She shrugged.

"That's not an answer."

She balled her hands into fists. "Fine." And then she paused, to choke off tears, or to think of how to put it into words, or neither, or both.

Eventually, she took a step forward, relaxed her hands, and took hold of mine. Any other day, I'd have worried about my palms sweating, and about what she would think, but it didn't matter, then. "Because there's nothing left for me to do. Because I'm tired. So you'll have to prop me up. Tell me you'll do it. Say 'I agree.'"

I wonder what would have happened, whether things would have gone some other way, if I'd have refused? Would she have stopped wearing plaid shirts and smelling like hay? Would there have been a future? An us?

I didn't want to look at her but somehow her eyes found mine. Nodding, I mumbled, "I agree." And then I bit my tongue, hard, because I wanted an excuse for the tears on my cheeks.

We walked to the field together, but with her out in front of me, as if she couldn't wait another minute to give it all up. When we arrived she could still stand on her own feet, but only just. She looked like a ragdoll, but girl-sized.

"Can you do this?" she asked. I guess she saw me gaping at the red wooden post she'd put in the ground. See, it wasn't really a post, but more of a cross, which both horrified me and gave me the urge to get down on my knees and pray. I guess that's usually when people like me decide to pray—when we're scared, when we've waited too long to do anything else. So even though I wasn't sure I believed in much of anything, I mouthed the words, 'Jesus, please tell my girl she doesn't have to do this.' I considered involving Buddha and Allah for good measure, too, but there wasn't enough time.

"Can you *do this*?" she asked again, with impatience on her face and urgency in her voice.

I nodded, and a moment later I was helping her position herself with her back to the post. Though she was nearly my height, she seemed to weigh nothing at all.

"Here," she said, and handed me the rope.

I took it, trying to ignore the sudden sense in my stomach of rotten food and old beer and too much heat. And then I tied her up, right around her belly, officially making her a prisoner to her obsessions, her fears, her self-imposed fate.

"There," I said. "It's done."

Reaching into her pockets, she nodded, then held up two smaller bits of twine. "Just one more thing."

"What?"

"My arms."

Somehow, I managed that too. And when it was finished, I took a tiny step back and looked her up and down. Trembling, I ran my fingers across the brim of her hat, wondering what had pushed her to that awful first step. Her eyes had never been so beautiful. But before I could tell her so, I watched her grow still and quiet. A hundred thoughts, all horrible and haunted, crossed my mind. I spoke none of them.

I waited an hour, maybe two, then walked back to the bunkhouse, by the longest route I knew. When I got there, I smoked a cigarette, then another, then spent the next hour or two ignoring the fact that I was too tough to cry.

The next year, the carnival took me to five or six cities, which all looked and felt empty against the backdrop of her absence. The year after that I retired from the world of duck ponds and prizes and fairgrounds. Time passed. Weeks, months, years. I figured out what she meant about love being a horror story. I spent some time as a mechanic. And then a janitor. And then as this and that and some other thing.

I stopped eating mandarin oranges and started collecting rubber ducks.

At first, I made the duck collection into a casual affair, passed it off as nostalgia for my younger years.

But now my desperation grows and I pretend less. I don't pretend to be smart and I don't care about looking foolish. I just hold the ducks in the palms of my hands and think 'If only.' If only they would turn into angry crows or possessed magpies or blue jays. If only they'd peck me to death, slow bit by slow bit, sinew by bloody sinew, and put me out of my misery. Please. *Please.*

Because at least I'd know: she had been right; she understood something I didn't; even now she is thinking of me.

When I'm not wishing for death, I dream of going back—back to that city along the Texas-Mexico border. And in my dreams, I find that field of corn where I abandoned her much too long ago. She's still there, standing among the knee-high stalks, her strawberry-blonde hair waving in the breeze. Her shirt has frayed, is all sun-worn and thin, but everything else about her is just the same. At first I walk, slow and carefree, as if I haven't been thinking of this moment for years, decades, an eternity. But as soon as she recognizes me, I can't resist and I run. I run, I run, *I run.* She's still attached to that wooden post, but she leans forward best she can, hastening our reunion by a foot. We laugh and cry and eventually I offer her an orange slice, and this time she takes it. And then I tell her I'm sorry, that I should have stayed, or begged her to come away with me.

When we kiss, she tastes of citrus. Not hay.

But if my dreams lie, as dreams so often do, if you don't always get what you want, if second chances are as rare as they seem . . . then she's too far gone. Or just *gone.* And each morning when I wake, it's with the knowledge that a corvidae-end would be better than confirming this reality.

TRUTH ABOUT CROWS

Craig Pay

"There's a crow at the door." Laykah was leaning back in her chair, peering out through the plexiglass window that overlooked their front yard. The sky outside was still stained with blood from the early morning First Sun light. "It's definitely a crow."

"Never mind that," her father said, without looking up from the bowl in front of him. He took another spoonful of porridge into his mouth, swallowed, then added, "I said—"

"Okay . . ." Laykah went back to poking at her own bowl of porridge.

She had never been one for breakfast, at least the manner of breakfast they could afford. Each day her father would slide two bowls of porridge onto the old dining table that he had built from recycled *Tàikōng Spaceways* packing crates: the last reminder of his arrival all those years ago aboard a long-distance stasis transport from Earth.

At the end of each meal he would clear the table again without saying a word about Laykah's bowl and how full it remained. She hated the porridge and the scratches of the tough little black husks against her throat. Her mother used to say she would make up for it later in the day and she always did, her stomach knotted and rumbling as the day waned and waxed through a half-dusk and false dawn and into an evening where both suns finally set and they would sit again to eat. Then Laykah would stuff her face until she couldn't eat anymore and slump back in her chair with her eyelids drooping.

The crow knocked at the front door and she once again leaned back in her chair. "Crow's still there."

"It'll be gone soon enough," her father said. He glanced at Laykah. "Amperage in the south field is down again."

"Blaumoles chewing at the wires."

"Take the hopper. Fix what you can."

"Hopper broke down weeks ago . . ." She hesitated for a moment before she added, "I keep telling you."

"Don't get smart with me young lady." He spooned down another mouthful. Pointed at her with his spoon. "Better get a move on."

"Hiring a crow would help," Laykah said.

He said nothing.

"Wouldn't draw much from the grid," she continued, "and we have the spares—"

"Enough!" he yelled out. "I'll hear no more of it."

She looked away. He thought she was too young to remember anything about her mother's passing. All that business with the other crow.

They continued to eat in silence. Laykah kept tilting her head to one side to listen but the knocking at the front door had stopped.

Laykah loaded up her backpack with all her tools, her multimeter, various power adaptors, cutters, collapsible shovel, loops of patching cable, armoured sheathing, her trusty fissile glue-gun. She pulled her goggles down over her head and left them dangling around her neck. Then she filled a flask with water from the gray-water recycler in the kitchen, sniffing at it before she screwed the cap into place. The water was starting to smell. The recycler would need looking at when she returned from the fields. She slid the flask into her pack and tested the weight of it all with one hand. Heavy but bearable.

She checked the dry bin on the kitchen countertop. It was empty. Her father would feign forgetfulness if asked and then he'd be in a bad mood for the rest of the week, so it wasn't worth the trouble. In truth, the lack of food was due to all the recent drops in power from the fields and the corresponding lack of payment from the municipal grid. A crow would help.

She shouldered her pack and listened to the house for a moment: just the distant sound of the wind playing at the shuttered windows upstairs but nothing else. Her father would be outside in one of the sub-station outbuildings servicing a step-up transformer or a circuit breaker or checking the lightning arrestors. She headed for the door and started to walk.

The road to the south wasn't much more than a narrow dirt track between the fields. Hoppers didn't need much to travel on, just a flat surface, but she was walking because they couldn't afford the hopper's annual service. The fields on either side were full with row after row of photovoltaic panels, each one glowing red from the reflected light from the First Sun as it cut across half the sky. In the distance, beyond the fields of panels, a line of blue-gray hills ran across the horizon.

Away from the house the wind began to pick up, blowing grit into her eyes, so she spat into each lens of her goggles, smeared her spit across the scratched plexiglass with one finger and pulled the goggles up into place. She couldn't see much of anything anymore but at least her eyes would stop hurting. She continued walking until a smear of white light on the horizon signalled the arrival of the Second Sun.

She stopped for a moment, shucked her pack from her shoulders and pulled her goggles down to hang around her neck. The collectors in the fields all around her were starting to come alive, servos grinding as they realigned to the fresh source of light. She fetched out her flask to take a drink and watched the Second Sun as it clambered over the horizon, feeling the heat of it on her face. That was when she saw the crow, a hundred paces further along the track.

Crows were made to look like people, but there something lopsided about this one. It was just standing at the side of the road with its ragged fake hair and patchwork clothes blowing in the thin wind.

She took another sip of water, re-shouldered her pack and walked closer to the crow. It didn't move. She could see that it was missing an arm—its right arm—which went partway towards explaining its unnatural look. This was one of the sorriest crows she had ever seen. Its clothes were a muted patchwork of faded browns and grays, its hair a jumble of old cables and plastic ties tangled together to form something that resembled a knot of dreadlocks.

"Hey!" she called out. "You the same crow as called at our place?"

The crow's head jerked around to face her. It said nothing. Nodded.

She asked, "What do you want?"

The crow's mouth opened and closed but no sound came out. It fell silent for long enough that she wondered whether it had finally broken down for good. Then it spoke in a dusty old voice laced with dirty static, "I need work scaring."

She shook her head. "My father won't allow it."

The crow said nothing.

Laykah hooked a thumb over her shoulder. "There's a town back there, two or three hours walk. Some folk there might have something for you."

The crow shook its head from side to side in stuttering, jerky movements. "Not enough charge. Stay here."

Laykah looked around then back to the crow. "And do what?"

Another long pause before the crow said, "Wait to die."

She mumbled, "Okay." Then walked past. Stopped again and looked back. The crow still hadn't moved. She walked back to it. "Can you walk? Just a few steps?" She pointed over to the nearest solar collector. "Over there?"

It nodded again.

She made it kneel next to one of the collectors and dropped her backpack to the ground. She dug out a set of keys and used them to pop a panel on the collector's control box. "Where's your line in?"

The crow bent forwards and used its one good hand to part the fake hair at the back of its head, revealing a deep socket.

She tried various different adaptors until she found one that would fit the crow's head socket. Then she spliced some cable, stripped away the silicone at either end to reveal the copper wires beneath, twisted the exposed strands with her fingers and fixed an adaptor to either end using a bright burst of thermal from her glue gun. She slotted one end of the improvised power cable into the back of the crow's skull and jacked the other into a spare socket inside the collector's control box. The crow's body jerked.

"Better?" she asked.

The crow said, "Yes."

She started to pack her things away again. "Unplug when you're topped off. Should be enough to get you to where you're headed."

"I need work," the crow said. "Scaring."

She stood and hoisted the backpack over her shoulders. Pulled her goggles up over her eyes. "I'm sorry, I can't." She turned to leave.

Laykah stopped again and turned around. Waited for the crow to catch up. It moved with a strange gait, obviously having problems with its balance because of its missing arm.

The Second Sun had moved past its zenith and was well on its way towards setting. She had already lost half the day.

As the crow reached her, it said in its dusty voice, "I am slow."

"It's fine," she said. "We're almost there."

They eventually reached the edge of the south fields. Straight away she could see the problem. A third of the collectors in the vast field had failed to turn to meet the Second Sun's light. Blaumoles.

The first settlers had coined the phrase "moles" obviously enough because they lived underground, digging tunnels, and "blau" meaning "blue" from some dead old Earth language. The moles weren't blue, they were gray, shelled, hairy things about a foot long with shovel claws and a face full of buckteeth, but they bled blue when you tried to kill them. And they had a taste for eating all the underground copper cables that linked the collectors to the grid.

She looked back at the crow. It had its head tilted to one side as if listening.

"I can hear them," the crow said. It raised its one good arm to point away across the field. "There."

"Okay," she said. "Get to work. I'll start patching."

She spent the next few hours popping panels from various collector control boxes, hooking up her multimeter to test the distances to the breaks, triangulating, pacing out, and digging down until she found the damage. She trimmed frayed cables, spliced in new sections, wrapped and heat-glued everything in new armoured sheathing. The Second Sun set and in the dim red light remaining she could just make out the crow standing still for the most part, moving every now and then to a different part of the field where it would go back to just standing.

She continued to work. Her flask was almost empty. The Second Sun was cresting the horizon as Laykah patched the last cable and scraped all the dirt back into the hole with her shovel. She stood and listened to the gentle clicking of servos all around here as the whole field of collectors moved together to track the Second Sun's light. She shouldered her pack and walked over to the crow, picking her way between the panels.

Close up, she could make out the crow's high-pitched ultrasonic keen at the very edge of her hearing. Older folks like her father couldn't hear anything at all and one day, when her own ears weren't quite so young, she'd be the same. But the blaumoles hated the noise. It drove them away.

She told the crow, "I'm going now."

The crow said nothing. Then its head jerked as it looked away, seemingly distracted, and it loped away across the field.

Laykah pulled her goggles up over her eyes and began to walk.

~

It was dark by the time she arrived home, only a single light on in the kitchen and her father waiting at the dining table. He said nothing at first, just pushed a plate of black bread and a bowl of now-cold soup towards her. He didn't like it when she arrived back after the First Sun had set even though the Second Sun would soon rise again.

He stood and pushed past her, mumbled something that sounded like a reprimand and was out from the kitchen before she realised it had been a compliment: "Good amperage from the south fields."

She sat and ate alone in silence.

The following morning they sat together and went through the usual porridge ritual.

Her father said, "South fields is still holding." His gaze was focused on the bowl in front of him. "You should stay here today." He stood up and left the room without saying anything else or clearing away the bowls.

That was about as close to a day off as she could ever hope for.

She placed the bowls into the sink, not quite sure what else to do with them as he usually dealt with all that. Then she grabbed her backpack, left the house and wandered over to the dusty old barn where they kept the hopper amidst various piles of junk. The hopper was a hover vehicle, a bike with a fan at the front and another at the rear. She spent a few hours working on it, replacing some corroded wiring, until she could hear the front and rear fan motors clicking as she thumbed the ignition. Not enough power to go anywhere right now but an overnight charge should help. She dragged the heavy charging cable over and plugged the hopper into the grid. She would take it for a test spin the following day.

The day was only half done. She glanced at the ladder that led up to the barn's loft. She wasn't allowed up there. Her father said it was too dangerous but she knew otherwise.

She shouldered her backpack, climbed the ladder and knelt before a tarpaulin-covered pile of junk. She pulled away the cover to reveal the mangled remains of a crow all covered in dust and feathers, its arms and legs twisted in contorted angles, the front of its head smashed in. She set about with her tools removing its right arm.

∾

The walk to the south fields seemed quicker than the previous day. She arrived as the Second Sun was just past its second zenith. She would easily get back in time for their evening meal without her father even realising that she had been away.

The crow had moved to another section of the field. The collectors were all still working, turning together. She picked her way through the field, between the panels. The crow ignored her, its head turning this way and that, listening to the ground.

"Can I check your charge?" she asked.

The crow jerked around to look at her. "Of course." It knelt and lifted a hand to the back of its head, pulling aside its fake hair.

Laykah plugged in her multimeter. The crow's power levels had dropped by only a few percentiles. It should be good for a week or so between charges.

"I have something else," she said, rummaging in her backpack for the arm she had detached from the remains of the crow in the barn.

She set about stripping back the wires at the crow's shoulder. She had to drill out the remains of the old shoulder joint to thermally dot-in the replacement arm. She connected up the wires as best she could.

As she twisted two wires together the crow's body jerked and she worried for a moment that she had dropped charge onto a control wire.

"Are you okay?" she asked.

The crow turned to face her. "Memories," it said. "High fragmentation. Recoverable. Continue?"

Her skin began to crawl. She sat back on her haunches. Crows used distributed systems all over their bodies for redundancy. They didn't just store memories in their heads.

She looked down at the arm and then back to the crow. "My mother?"

The crow nodded.

"How long to recover?" she asked.

The crow was silent for a moment before it said, "Several hours."

"Fine. Do it."

She continued to work at all the wires until the crow was able to move its new arm and flex its fingers. Then she packed her things and stood. Helped the crow to its feet. She told it to continue working. "I'll come back tomorrow."

"You were out at the south fields again today," her father said.

Laykah hesitated with a chunk of black bread halfway towards her mouth. They were sitting at the dining table in the kitchen. She shrugged. "Yes." She took a bite and began to chew.

"I don't mind," he said. "Just tell me when you're heading off, so I know when to expect you back."

He had already finished his own food and was leaning back in his chair, eyes fixed on her.

"What did you do?" he asked. "We're still getting good amperage from the south fields. Did you double up on armoured sheathing? I've told you before, that's too expensive."

She swallowed the bread. Shook her head. "No—I just—I don't know."

He was frowning now. Still staring at her. He knew there was something she wasn't telling him. She decided not to say anything in case it made the situation worse.

"Then what?" he said. "I've been down there a dozen times before now and the cabling never holds out for more than a few hours."

"I took on that crow."

Silence. When her father spoke, his voice was slow and deliberate, "You did what?"

Laykah looked away.

"After everything that happened to your mother," her father continued. "You brought a crow into our house back then and you've gone and done it again!"

"This isn't the same."

He slammed a hand down onto the table, rattling the plates and cups then stood and stomped out of the kitchen, slamming the door behind him. Noise from upstairs.

She wanted to go after him to tell him this was a different crow. That there was nothing he could have done back then. Memories of her childhood: her mother lying in bed for three days straight, her body soaked in sweat, wracked in the pains of childbirth. A little brother for Laykah that would never be born. Her father had taken the hopper to the nearest town to bring back a doctor, but he was gone for hours. Laykah's mother eventually told her: *"Go be a honey. Fetch the crow."* Later that evening, her father returned home, went upstairs and started shouting. He dragged the crow, still clutching the pillow it used on her mother, out into the yard and smashed in its head with an old lumber axe.

The kitchen door flew open. Her father stood there with the same axe held again in both hands. "Stay here!" Then he was gone, out of the house and away into the darkness.

Laykah put her backpack on and went out to the old barn, pulling the doors open wide.

She climbed the ladder and yanked at the remains of the old crow's battered head until it came away in her hands. A crow might store its memories all about its body but it still needed a mouth to speak. She shoved the head into her backpack and went back down the ladder.

She clambered onto the hopper. Tightened the straps on her goggles and tugged them down over her eyes, ignoring the way the straps pulled at her hair.

She thumbed the ignition and both fans burst into life, stirring up a storm of dust and debris that whirled about the barn. She gave the engines a few extra revs. The hopper jumped off the ground and began to slew sideways until she brought it back in line again.

Then she red-lined the engines and the hopper took off, leaving the barn behind. She took the east road to avoid her father, grit bouncing off her goggle lenses and stinging against her forehead. This way was longer but she should still arrive in plenty of time. After a while the Second Sun began to rise, casting its pale light across all the glass-covered fields whipping past on either side.

Laykah found the crow standing in the middle of the south collector field. She parked the hopper and pulled the goggles down around her neck. She sniffed and spat on the ground. She would be coughing up dust for days.

As she approached the crow, its head jerked around and it said, "I have the memories. Shall I proceed to play them for you? Audio only."

She wanted to sit down and spend hours listening to the crow, hearing her mother's second-hand words. Instead, she said, "We don't have time. Not yet. One day. Can you take all of the memories into your own head? Keep them there for later?"

The crow nodded in its jerky way.

"Good," she said. "Do it. Do it right now."

The crow tilted its head to one side and then it said, "It is done."

Laykah rummaged around in her backpack. "I—I have to do something." She pulled out a cutter and the remains of the other crow's battered head from her backpack. "I'm sorry."

The crow knelt down and bowed its head. Laykah set to work.

She had no idea whether this would work or if her father would stop to wonder why the crow wasn't moving as it knelt there in the field. Would he recognise the same head on this crow as the one he destroyed a handful of years ago? She wouldn't know whether her plan had worked until the following morning when the two of them sat together again at the dining table with him lecturing to her about all the wrongs of crows. On her way back home she would bury this crow's head in a field where it would remain hidden until her father had passed away and all the fields belonged to her. Then she would find another crow body for this one. And she would listen to all of its memories.

TWO STEPS FORWARD

Holly Schofield

I eased myself down off the running board of the '28 Hudson sedan then laid a hand on the hood in mute sympathy for its overheated pistons. A quick buttoning-up of my topcoat and a tug on my fedora and I felt ready to approach the farmhouse.

The old woman on the veranda watched me as I drew close. Flyaway gray hair surrounded a narrow, clever face, faded housedress atop rubber boots; she was as much of a hodgepodge as I used to be. The late model Stewart Warner radio perched on the windowsill shimmied with "The Spell of the Blues." I hummed along as the saxophones swooped and soared.

The old woman fingered the jumble of items on her lap as if looking for a weapon and I stopped a few feet from the bottom step of the porch.

"Afternoon, ma'am." I tipped my hat, not too far, and put my hands in my pockets. "I won't take up much of your time. Your husband built that famous automated scarecrow, am I right?" At her tightening mouth, I quickly added, "I'm not a reporter, just an admirer. I saw that scarecrow ace the dance marathon at the Playland Pavilion in Montreal last winter. Truly hep to the jive." The ballroom's mirrored walls reflecting the graceful moves of the dark-suited figure, hands as clever as Frisco twirling a chiffon-clad partner—a sight worth seeing, all right. The old woman grunted and picked up a dirty rag. She poured something golden and syrupy over it from a pickle jar, and began rubbing a coaster-sized metal disc—a flywheel? a gear?—with more vigor than necessary.

The sun beat down on my hat and heavy coat. Manitoba in August could cook a person's innards. Common courtesy would be to invite me onto the porch. She said nothing. I did as she'd expect and walked over to the shade of the big maple that crowded against the railing.

When she finally spoke, her voice grated like sand in a pocketwatch. "Yup, he built that thing." The words hung on the dust-filled air. She put down the disc and squinted into the shade where I stood. "He's dead and gone. I think you mebbe know that."

She'd lied with ease. Getting her to do what I needed would be harder than mastering the Lindy Hop.

"I heard that, ma'am, and you have my sympathies," I said, continuing to play innocent. "Can I ask, why didn't he build more than the one?" It had bothered me for ages and I'd thought about it the whole six-hour drive out here from Winnipeg. Why not make another of the marvelous two-stepping scarecrows? Dozens? Hundreds? The floorboards of the dance halls from here to Toronto could quiver from the beat of a thousand metallic toes.

"Why should I tell you about Abe's affairs? You a tax man?"

"No, ma'am. I'm not from the tax office." Not even close.

"The bank, then. I s'pose you're here to hand me a late mortgage notice? I already got two."

"No, ma'am. I'm not from the bank. Just interested, is all. Music is my life."

"Well, even if you were foreclosing, there's nothing here you want anyway. No one will buy this land no more. With Abe gone, I can't put in a wheat crop and I sold off all the cows. No equipment worth a red cent, neither. Don't go thinking there's a fancy workshop here. That mechanical boy was constructed from cast-off junk: washing machine parts, broken wooden pipes, ball joints from the old John Deere's drive shaft. Junk, all junk." She paused and spat over the side of the railing. "Damn thing never did a decent stroke of work keeping the birds off my vegetables."

"With respect, ma'am, I heard the mechanical man was the cat's whiskers at hoofing around the joint, giving those wingèd pests the bum's rush."

My poetical words must have painted a fine picture—her shoulders relaxed slightly, like a dance marathoner on the second day. She finished polishing the gear and laid it on the old wicker table beside her, next to a tin can heaped with ball bearings. She picked up a smaller gear from her lap, with cogs the size of babies' teeth, and turned it over and over. "The head, doncha know, was an old tea kettle. The handle was busted so it got soldered back onto the side— made the funniest-looking ear you ever saw." The side of her mouth quirked up.

From my place in the shadows, I nodded several times. "The copper sheen made him look like he perspired when he danced." A certain swanky Winnipeg dance hall lit up my memory, the figures whirling in bright dresses and suits, foxtrotting to *Brother, Can You Spare a Dime*. The orchestra had so enchanted me that, at times, I had been oblivious to the torture of that twenty-six day marathon: the cruel catcalls from the paying audience, the MC's brutal "sprint" contests, the total exhaustion of my partner as she slept standing upright against my rigidly-held shoulder through the nights. Like all my partners, she kept her energy for dancing, not talking, so I never learned much about her beyond her name.

"He covered his head up, pretty quick, I heard tell, when he bummed his way east outta here. Got it coated with that newfangled Bakelite. Nobody could tell he wasn't a person except for the steam coming out his nose spout." She peered over at me. "How'd you know his head was copper?"

Jeez Louise, call me a chowderhead! She might be near-sighted but she wasn't dim. I changed the subject fast. "One of the gossip rags said he got the nose fixed too, just redirected the steam to vent out several places on his body. The girls found him plenty steamy, all right. A real 'Lothario from Ontario.'" I laughed and was relieved to see the corner of her mouth twitch up further.

"Heard he won all the marathon contests from here to Montreal," she said, gruffly, leaning back enough to make the wicker creak. "Guess nobody else *could* make another one, or they would have—just to get the prize money."

Like a roadhouse gambler closing in on his patsy, it was time to show a little of my hand. If we didn't come to an understanding, all this was for naught.

"Nobody has your skill, ma'am." I let that sentence lie there, overlaying the chirp of the grasshoppers and the waltz that now drifted out the window, and took a big gulp from my hip flask.

The old woman cackled. "Smart as a whippersnapper, aren't you? Yeah, I built the damn thing. Kept me busy the winter before Abe passed, just like my new radio. Didn't want to admit to it, after the reporters started coming around. I started off real simple. I only wanted to keep the sparrows off my strawberries and such. Then he began dancing, slick as oil. Twirling around in the moonlight, all graceful and smooth, in that wrinkled-up swallowtail coat the undertaker gave me. After a few months, I stuck an old axle kingpin in his ankles so he could bend in all the right places. Never got a thank you." She leaned back and put her hands behind her. I couldn't quite read her expression.

I pictured the scene as a crow might see it: the scarecrow high-stepping under the moon, tails flapping, twisting like the hepcat he would become. NBC's Palmolive Hour alive with sweet jazz, the hopeful scent of ripening tomatoes, and the moonlight playing among the carrot fronds. The scarecrow tap dancing madly to "California, Here I Come" as it blared out the window of the farmhouse he was never, ever invited into.

She leaned forward, studying me. "Nice coat," she said. I straightened the collar, pleased she had noticed. Camel-hair, with leather-covered buttons, it had been the feature in the Eaton's window all spring and had cost me the moola from my last three marathons. She spun a gear on her finger, round and round. "Bet it's hard to keep the coal dust off it."

We understood each other all right. I touched my chest with my gloved hands then held them out to her, in mute recognition of her statement.

Her voice rasped. "That mechanical boy never appreciated the oil I rubbed in his joints, the coal I shovelled beneath his boiler, the spot-welding when he broke a toe. He just up and run off, right before harvest. The birds poked holes in most of the squash before the sun had set that day. By golly, I should have made one leg shorter so he could only walk in circles."

"Perhaps," I said, "the radio is to blame."

"The radio?" She dropped the gear with a clank. "Well, I never! The radio!"

"Like peeking through a keyhole day after day, never being able to open the door. He wanted to see everything for himself, touch everything, live everything. You name it, he wanted it. Jam sessions, mellow rhythms, swell fellows and grooving chicks. He wanted it all."

"Horsefeathers!"

I jammed my hands in my pockets. Johnny Green's *Easy Come, Easy Go* finished its chorus and slid into a long bridge, silky as cream.

The old woman swayed a bit to the beat then caught herself. She must have cut quite a rug in her younger days. "A bum, a wastrel, that's what he is," she said, as if she'd said it many times before.

The wailing horns were drawing me in. I clenched my fists harder and tightened my knee joints, fighting the urge. I had to make her see. "Perhaps he wanted to do more than chase birds away, as if he was a deuce of tin pie plates banging in the wind. Perhaps he wanted to earn you some lettuce when Abe was huddled in bed with scarlet fever. But perhaps,"—I faltered then continued—"you'd rather let the bank seize the farm than take help from me."

Bridges burned, I stepped out into the sunlight, swept off my fedora, and let the sun beat down on my beige Bakelite-covered head. I opened my coat and took out the prize money from Toronto's Nationwide Super Marathon, laying the thick wad of cash on the top step of the porch.

The old woman stood up, heedless of the gears, springs, and other clockworks tumbling from her lap. She took the two steps necessary to grab the money and turned away, rubbing her eyes. Her gnarled hand wrenched open the screen door and she disappeared into the dimness beyond. The door slammed behind her so loudly the starlings took off from the clothesline in indignation.

I took another swig from my flask, the last of the kerosene failing to ease the tightness in my throat. Steam from several of my apertures drifted faintly up toward the gutters. A thank you would have been too much but I'd hoped for a friendly smile or a hi de ho. And a cup of her special lubricating blend would have hit the spot before I drove my car down the dirt track back to the highway, back to the dance halls, back to the bleak faces of the marathoners. I'd learned that dance floors didn't sparkle so much after the glitter dust got trampled. I was a scarecrow with a lot of dashed hopes, an excellent sense of rhythm, and a chest that was as hollow as a certain famous tinman.

My hand had cranked open the Hudson's door handle when the old woman hailed me, something bright in her hand. The crows mocked from the maple as I returned to the veranda, my new wingtip shoes causing aches in places I didn't know I had.

"Take the damn key ring," she said. "Go out to the smaller barn next to the coal shed." She waved a hand, impatient at my slowness in mounting the steps. "You need to wind them counterclockwise, light the kerosene-soaked coal, squirt all their joints with a drop or two of lubricant, and then explain to them about . . . well, about everything."

The keys jangled from my glove-clad fingers. "Them?"

"The other scarecrows. There's six ready in the barn and half a one in the workshop that's not finished yet. It's been a slow summer." She trudged back into the house, lifting her heels very slightly in time to *Sweet Sue, Just You.*

ONLY THE LAND REMEMBERS

Amanda Block

The Crows are gathering.

Grace is curled up on the window seat upstairs, her arms around her knees, her fingers picking at the loose hem of her sleeve. This is the only spot in the house where she can watch them; it is just high enough to see over the town wall.

They are smudged in the crisscross of panes, the glass distorting the almost-human shape of them, so that if Grace moves her head even a little, they seem to lurch from side to side. But even blurred those dark spirits are unmistakable, and she knows that, for now at least, they stand perfectly still beyond the border.

It calms her to sit here, taking stock of them: three by the gate, eight in the orchard, the rest away in the fields. Yesterday, there were two dozen; now she counts twenty-nine.

After a while, her vision relaxes and she leans forward, a cold kiss lingering where her brow touches the window.

"Shoo," Grace whispers, her breath fogging the glass. "Get away. *Shoo.*"

᷾

(Seven days earlier)

Once the cursed spirits of the Untamed are Gathering (meaning their number has reached over a score), the town must request volunteers for a Clearing.

153

Those eligible for the Clearing must be of appropriate standing within the community, therefore the following persons need not come forward:
Those under the age of sixteen
Women who are with child or have lately borne a child
Men owning more than ten hectares of farmland
Men of the church
Members of the council
Physicians, healers and those practiced in medicine

As Father Francis read from the leather-bound Charter, Grace waited alongside the other volunteers: sickly Mr. West; the widow Elizabeth from across the way; an older woman she didn't know. They kept glancing sideways at her, but she already knew she looked out of place, standing with them on the steps of the town hall.

Grace was third to draw. She has since tried to remember why she picked that particular strand, and sometimes recalls it had a greenish hue that appealed to her, as though there were some life in it yet, but that might have been something she invented later. What she remembers most is the leap of her heart, as the straw slid easily from the priest's fist, small and smooth and sharp.

She hadn't planned it, but she thrust the straw high into the air, for the entire crowd to see. Then as the whispers of her name rippled to the very edges of the town square, she murmured a fierce prayer of thanks.

Father Francis stepped forward, closing the Charter. "Let it be known who has been selected for the Clearing," he said. "Honored by—"

With a moan, the widow shook her head. "Father, she's a child. We'll choose again . . ."

Mr. West and the other woman both murmured their agreement.

No, Grace thought, looking anxiously to the priest. But he simply went on as though no interruption had taken place.

"Honored by God, feared by the Untamed, Grace Palmer is the Scarecrow."

⁓

"Gracie?"

As she turns from the window, the dark shapes of the Crows remain in her vision for a few seconds, imprinting themselves over the figure of her father.

"It's almost time," he says.

She shuffles from the seat, her progress made awkward by the weight of her dress.

"You look very fine," he mumbles, gesturing towards it. "Although are you sure, considering—?"

She holds up a hand to stop him. "I'm doing God's work," she says, trying to smile. "No matter what happens, I want to—" She stops, unsure how to say it.

"You'll shine like a pearl underneath," he tells her.

Grace looks down at the loose thread of her sleeve and a silence falls between them, during which her father shifts his weight from foot to foot, the floorboards protesting beneath his shoes.

"You remember your promise?" he asks eventually.

"Yes."

More silence follows, although this time it is Grace who speaks first.

"I think I'd like a little time outside—with Mother's tree—before we go."

He nods, as though he has been expecting this. "I'll fetch you in a few minutes."

Grace calls him back as he heads for the stairs.

"Father? Perhaps I could have a little longer? I need to say my prayers."

When he looks back at her, his expression is almost distressed.

"Even tonight?" he asks.

"Especially tonight."

❧

(Seven days earlier)

Grace's father had not relinquished his grip on her elbow the whole way home. She allowed herself to be marched back, inwardly preparing for his reaction, as she had been ever since volunteering.

"Why did you do it?" he demanded, as soon as they were inside.

"It was my choice, father."

He gripped at her shoulders. It didn't hurt, but it forced her to face him—to see the shock and pain in his expression.

"Did you not see the others? They're old and ill and alone, whereas you—"

"I'm of age!"

"—you have your whole life ahead of you!"

"I'm of age," Grace repeated stubbornly.

He let her go, slumping into a chair and shaking his head just as the widow Elizabeth had done.

"I don't understand, Gracie. How could you do this to yourself? How could you do this to *me*?"

She knelt at his side, gazing up at him and gripping at his arm with both her hands.

"Father, don't you see? I'm young, I'm strong, and I'll face them with God in my heart."

He grimaced at this, just as he had taken to grimacing in church.

"They won't take me, I'm sure of it," Grace went on. "I'll be one of the ones who comes back—I'll come back to you."

Later, when his panic had abated, he had begun to prepare the potatoes for dinner, hacking at each of their skins until he grew impatient and tossed them into earthy water.

"Can you promise me?" he said, after neither of them had spoken for a long while.

"Sorry?"

"If you're so sure that God will protect you," he went on, glowering at the potato in his hand, "can you promise me you'll return, no matter what happens with those—those creatures?"

"Of course," she said, without hesitation. "I promise."

He let out a humorless laugh. "Just like that? You're so certain?"

"I'm certain of God."

He frowned at her for a moment, and then turned his attention back to the potatoes.

"You're just like your mother," he said. Then, nodding over at the empty chair beside him, he added, "And look at all the good it did her."

⁓

The cloud is low this evening; it renders the granite walls and cobbled roads dull, lacking their usual shine, and will choke the sunset when it comes.

On her father's arm, Grace is walking down the same streets that lead to the market, or her old school, or dances at the town hall. Only now they are different. This route seems colder, grayer, and there is not a soul in sight.

Maybe it is better this way. Since she was chosen, people she has known all her life have treated her differently—almost fearfully. Of course, they have smiled at her, and some have even offered her their gratitude, but then they have turned away too quickly, or else she has heard them whispering before she is out of earshot.

Still, it is strange, this empty town. It is almost as though the situation is reversed, and she is the only one remaining within its walls tonight. She thinks about commenting as much to her father, but decides against it. He has not uttered a word since they left the house, and she fears he will not speak at all until they reach the church.

∾

(Three days earlier)

"The Eleventh Song of the Crossing"

This land of ours was cruel and wild,
Before us, long ago:
Ruled o'er by those with souls defiled
E'en God did them forgo.

But those Untamed, they should have known
That evil has a price:
They bred and fought amongst their own
And perished from their vice.

(Oh-la-la, oh-la-la, oh-la-la, oh!)

Our ancestors, who wanted more,
Across seas they did roam,
Until they spied this distant shore;
A place they could call home.

They built each house and ev'ry street
To spread God's holy word.
But in the earth beneath their feet
The restless Untamed stirred.
(Oh-la-la, oh-la-la, oh-la-la, oh!)

Dark shadows then began to swarm,

And growth beneath them froze,
So for this plague and their dark form,
Our people called them Crows.

Those dead Untamed had cursed this ground,
O'er it, they'd cast this spell:
And that is how we all were bound
To spirits straight from Hell.

(Oh-la-la, oh-la-la, oh-la-la, oh!)

Our town, it was held in their thrall,
Until a man of worth
Went out one eve beyond the wall,
To drive them from this earth.

With torch and cloak he stood all night,
And 'round him Crows did throng,
But though he was made pale with fright,
His heart was pure and strong.

(Oh-la-la, oh-la-la, oh-la-la, oh!)

The townsfolk woke with great concern
They feared the good man dead,
But with the dawn he did return,
And all the Crows had fled.

Thus this good soul who'd faced the horde,
His courage was proclaimed:
That righteous man, blessed by the Lord,
The Scarecrow he was named.

(Oh-la-la, oh-la-la, oh-la-la, oh!)

During one of her vigils at the window seat, Grace found herself humming. It was many years since she'd learned that ditty—it was taught to children starting school and church, along with the other Songs of the Crossing—but she found she could still recite it by heart.

It was comforting, she supposed; more hopeful than the other stories surrounding the first Scarecrow. In one of the tales she'd heard later, he had returned to the town different, troubled, and within a year he had hanged himself from the rafters of the town hall.

Another less comforting thought occurred to her: the Crows always returned, in the end.

Most of the town is gathered in the churchyard when Grace and her father arrive. She kneels before them and Father Francis places a hand on her head.

"Blessed are we who gather here this evening, to see God's child, Grace Palmer, depart for her holy task . . ."

The fingers of the priest are trembling, so much so that it distracts Grace from what is being said.

". . . Amen," he says at last.

"Amen," the crowd replies.

Father Francis bends down, picks up a fistful of soil, and smears a little across Grace's forehead, first down, then across. Afterwards he opens his arms to include the watching people.

"I now invite you all to help prepare Grace for the Clearing . . ."

The crowd surges forward before he has finished speaking. Suddenly, Grace is surrounded by bodies, and hands are in her hair, on her dress, even at her shoes, pulling and tearing and scratching. There is earth too, great clumps of it, being smeared into her clothes and skin and scalp. It slips down her collar, into her ears and almost to the corners of her eyes. But she bears it all, silent and still, though the fervor of the crowd is unnerving.

"Enough," booms her father's voice above the noise.

The priest nods and everyone draws back. Then he hands Grace the torch and drapes the heavy, tattered cloak over her shoulders.

"Go," he whispers, in her soil-clogged ear.

Shoo.

Grace stares down at her feet as she begins to walk, unwilling to focus on the crowd. She does not need to see their faces to know that she is transformed: her dress is torn, some of it ripped clean away; her hair is tangled and loose; her whole body smeared with earth and grit and even a little blood. Indeed, though this is how the ritual goes, she burns with the shame of what she has become: barbaric, savage, Untamed.

Scarecrow.

∼

(Two days earlier)

"I've already told you, there is nothing I can do."

"You can choose again, pick someone else!"

Summoned by the raised voices downstairs, Grace crept from her room, avoiding the floorboards that creaked.

"That's impossible, it goes against everything in the Charter. She was chosen, it is done."

"She's too young!"

"She's old enough to volunteer, it says in the Charter—"

"Hang the Charter, she's a child!"

Grace slid into a sitting position at the top of the stairs, half touched and half shocked by how her father was speaking to the priest.

"You know they're your responsibility," he went on, "these—these Crow demons, whatever you want to call them. The church should be protecting our children from them, not sending them out to do battle!"

"But we can't, you know that. We've tried everything: holy water, sacrifice, even exorcism, it's all in—" Father Francis seemed to think better of mentioning the Charter again. "It's all recorded."

There was a long silence. Grace drew her shawl tighter over her nightdress and waited.

"In helping to preserve the town from the legacy of the Untamed, Grace will be doing God's work, Mr. Palmer. It is an honor for your family."

"If she goes, I'll have no family left."

The priest had no response to this, so pressed on with a different line of argument. "You have to remember, they can come back, the Scarecrows. William Bell wasn't taken, thirty years ago. I know he moved on, but by all accounts his farm prospers. And Ellen Turner's still here—she returned, didn't she?"

"Not whole!" Grace's father roared. "Not with her wits! We all saw the state she was in—heard the wicked things she said. Heaven knows what they did to her. Heaven knows what they'll do to my Gracie . . ."

His voice broke. Grace put her arms around one of the banisters, resting her cheek against the cold wood.

"I'm sorry, Mr. Palmer," said the priest. "I know your faith has wavered since your wife's illness, but perhaps I can suggest some verses that might offer you some comfort?"

He didn't receive a reply, and a few minutes passed before he spoke again.

"Otherwise, I must return to the church. There is much to be done."

Evidently deciding to let himself out, the priest appeared in the hallway. He paused at the door, as though sensing a pair of eyes on his back, and looked up. Seeing Grace, he nodded, and she nodded back.

Then, before her father could find her, she ran back along the corridor and into her bed. Her feet were cold against one another as she wriggled deeper under the blankets, but even when she stopped shivering, sleep would not come.

The crunching of the gate being closed and bolted behind her seems to echo in Grace's ears. She has only ventured beyond the wall five times in her life—and never without a farmer or during a Gathering.

I have been chosen, she remembers, as she forces herself forward. *I'll face them with God in my heart.*

She adjusts the cloak around her shoulders and tries to focus on the land, hoping it will incite something in her stronger than fear. The hard ground on which she walks is bruised with blackened soil, as though many fires have been recently stamped out. This is where the Crows have stood, and the scorched-looking earth will be barren for generations to come.

Grace's fingers curl into fists. *This is ours,* she thinks. *Shoo.*

Her conviction last for just a few minutes, after which she looks to the horizon and is struck by nausea so strong her whole body sways. She can see them now, just ahead: tall and still, they are like standing stones silhouetted against the darkening sky.

(One day earlier)

"Ellen? Ellen, dear? You have a visitor."

Grace had been very young at the time of the last Clearing, but the memory of the proud female figure clad in rags had stayed with her. She realized now that this is what she had been expecting—a Scarecrow—but the woman sitting on the bed was small and meek.

Her soft blonde hair was plaited neatly down her back and her girlish dress looked wrong on her middle-aged body.

"Ellen, this is Grace Palmer," went on Mrs. Turner. "She's come to see you."

Ellen looked up, but said nothing. Her eyes were very green.

"Hello," said Grace, with an awkward wave of her hand.

"Have a seat," said Mrs. Turner, indicating Grace should take the chair next to the bed. Then, looking nervous, she said, "Ellen dear, Grace has come to ask you about being the Scarecrow."

Ellen blinked. "Scarecrow," she repeated.

"That's right." Mrs. Turner looked encouraged. "You remember when you were the Scarecrow, and you saved the whole town from the Crows? Do you remember that, my darling?"

Another blink. "Crows."

Mrs. Turner reached forward, took her daughter's hand. "You went out there, the bravest girl in the land, and in the morning, you came back to us, didn't you? You came back to your family."

Her voice wavered. Grace fidgeted, recalling her father's words: *Not whole. Not with her wits.*

"Now Grace here has volunteered, just like you did. And she wants to talk to you about it."

Ellen looked between her mother and Grace several times.

"Scarecrow," she said again.

Mrs. Turner sighed.

"Please," Grace found herself saying, "please, tell me what it's like. Do I just stand there? Do I pray?"

Ellen shrank back, apparently unnerved at being addressed directly by a stranger. Mrs. Turner hardly seemed to notice: she was looking at Grace with almost the same expression with which she looked at her daughter.

"I wish you'd come sooner," she murmured. "Some days she's better than others."

164

Grace didn't say so, but she wished it too. She had never thought to find herself in the Turner house—nobody did. Only children would linger outside its door, competing as to how far they could run up its path before they lost their nerve.

As the three of them lapsed into silence, Grace looked around. Ellen's room—the whole house, in fact—was far from the cobwebby haunt of her imaginings. It was bright and clean and full of cooking smells. It was, she realized, just like her own house.

"I should go," she said, when no one had spoken for some time. "My father doesn't know I'm here . . ."

But as she rose from the chair, Ellen suddenly lunged forward. Grace gave a cry of shock and fear as the woman's fingernails cut into the skin of her wrist.

"Ellen, no!"

But the woman paid her mother no heed. She yanked at Grace's arm, pulling her down so that their faces were very close.

"I'll tell you," whispered Ellen. "You have to live through it. Do you see?"

"Y-yes," Grace stammered, grateful for the encouragement yet desperate to reclaim her arm.

"You'll live through it, you must!"

"I want to—I want to come back. Please, tell me how . . ."

But apparently Ellen had said enough, for she sat back on the bed. Releasing Grace's wrist, she gazed up at the ceiling and slowly raised her arms.

For the first time, Mrs. Turner looked stern. "Now, Ellen, not this again . . ."

But Ellen didn't hear her: she was humming a low, sorrowful tune that Grace didn't recognize as a hymn or a Song of the Crossing. She swayed a little as she sang, her arms still outstretched.

"I'm sorry, but we'll get no more out of her now," Mrs. Turner said.

Nodding, Grace followed her to the door, unable to resist taking one last look back at the other Scarecrow. *Will I be stronger than her?* Grace wondered. *Even if they do not take me, will I return whole?*

Ellen, oblivious to these questions, continued to hum until suddenly—with no warning at all—she fell into a heap on the bed. Grace stared: slumped and still, the collapsed figure looked like a puppet whose strings had been cut.

⁓

The Crows are different up close. From the window, Grace had thought them like shadows or black mist, but now she sees there is a density to their darkness, as though the Untamed ripped deep holes in the world before they left it.

At her approach, the Crows have begun to move. It is a slow, rippling motion, quite unlike the flapping of their namesakes. Grace turns, trying to keep them all in her sightline, but this is impossible: there are far more than twenty-nine now, all of them drifting in different directions. By the time Grace has realized they are forming a circle, she is trapped at its center.

She turns on the spot, her breath coming fast and short: she is in a nightmarish version of a children's game, and she doesn't know the rules.

Do I just stand there? Do I pray?

But poor, mad Ellen hadn't said; perhaps she hadn't even known. Grace tightens her grip on the torch, trying to swallow the panic rising in her throat.

"My name is Grace Palmer," she says, surprised by how loud she sounds in the breezeless night. "I am the Scarecrow, and I have come to clear you from this land."

She braces herself for a response—an attack, even—but nothing happens. Around her, the Crows are silent and unmoving. Do they know who she is, what she is saying? Grace isn't sure, and somehow this spurs her on.

"Crows, cursed creatures of the Untamed, in the good Lord's name I ask—I *demand*—you leave this place!"

The Crows remain still. Grace's voice rises to a shout.

"This is our land! This is our home! You cannot—"

The circle shifts as though each creature has shivered. While Grace hesitates, the largest of the Crows—one far taller than her—begins drifting forward, right into the center of the ring. Its emptiness is sickening: what would happen, she wonders, if she were to fall right through it? Gasping, Grace backs away, forgetting there are creatures behind her too.

The dark shape continues to advance, paying no heed to the torch with which Grace is slashing at the air between them. Something is growing from the side of its bulk, something long and grasping, almost like an arm.

"Get back!" Grace cries, as it tries to clutch at her. "On behalf of God Almighty, I—"

I watched them approach, that day they came back. I stood at the wall and I studied each of their faces. Those men were pale, so much so I thought them sickly; beneath those strange, heavy clothes, I imagined their bodies to be as weak as children's. They did not even carry weapons, other than their sticks.

Still, I hesitated. We had never seen such men in this land, and doubt filled my heart, as though all the earth and every god was warning me: send them away.

But we had made a bargain. With gestures and pictures drawn in the earth, we had agreed to trade with these strangers. And what was the harm in that? What damage could these fragile figures possibly inflict?

So I raised my arm, I gave the signal: open the gate.

The Crow lets go of Grace and returns to its position in the circle. She staggers, staring wide-eyed at the gloomy field and her dark, still companions. For a moment, she had been somewhere else: the town—her home—on a different day. She had been someone else too.

She stoops for the torch she has dropped, which is sputtering on the blackened ground. Her hands are shaking so much she can barely pick it up. What has she just seen? A memory? Some unholy vision?

"What are you showing me, Crow?" she asks the creature that gripped at her. Her voice sounds stronger than she feels.

But it is a different member of the circle that responds: it drifts towards her, reaching out.

I was to stay inside when the strangers returned. My husband told me so, even though—oh!—how I wanted to see them! He said their skin was milk-white, and their eyes like clear pools of water, sparkling in the sunlight.

I did as I was told until the shouting began, and then I crept from my chair and peered out of the door. A figure was limping towards me: my neighbor, his eyes bulging with terror, his hands clawing at a slash to his stomach.

He fell to his knees, and I started towards him, but he shook his head.

"Run!" he choked, through a mouthful of blood. "Run!"

And as he collapsed, the thunder began; great bursts of it, even though there was no storm.

Grace has her hands over her ears as the Crow releases her, the banging loud in her head. When it stops, she looks up.

"You go—get back!" she says, though the creature is already reclaiming its place in the circle.

The torch is on the ground once more, but Grace doesn't bother to retrieve it. Instead, she runs her hands through her dirty, tangled hair, trying to make sense of it all. Who had she just been? Had that man died? Was it even a man? His color and features and clothes were different from her own . . .

It doesn't matter, Grace tells herself, *it wasn't real.*

But another Crow is coming.

The noise from their sticks was like nothing I had ever heard. It was louder than the screams of the women, louder even than our battle cry, as we rallied for the fight.

The strangers were scattering, using the confusion caused by their weapons to spread themselves through the town. I spotted two ahead, and with a bellow of fury, I pelted after them, my spear aloft.

I do not know whether it found its target before I fell. After the thunder-noise, I was scrabbling on the ground, clawing at the pain in my leg, and I couldn't remember if I had thrown it.

A stranger approached from behind and kicked me down when I tried to rise. He pointed the end of his stick at my face: it was a hollow, smoking tunnel, and it smelt of fire and death.

Grace jerks back.

"Stop it!" she shouts, batting in vain at the retreating form of the Crow. "This didn't happen, that isn't my town!"

But the apparitions, the possessions—whatever they are—do not feel untrue: the pain and the panic is far too real.

It was too late to escape; I could hear them surrounding the house. I only had time to bundle my boy under some rags, pleading with him to stay quiet, before the strangers knocked down my door.

I had been skinning a rabbit, and the knife was still in my hand, but there were three of them, so it was easy enough to smack it from my fingers while I was distracted.

When I screamed, they pounced. One of them came up behind me, seized my hair and pushed me face-first towards the table. As I tasted blood, I felt his body press down on mine, and his hands grip at the back of my thighs.

I froze then. And throughout it all, I stared at that pile of old cloth in the corner, willing it to stay as still and silent as me.

"No, please!" Grace is sobbing now. "Please, stop! Why are you doing this?"

But the Crows don't reply; they just keep coming.

My brother had always been strong and quick, and he fought until the end, in spite of his wounds. It took four of them to wrestle him to the ground, and even then he writhed and spat like a snake.

It was dishonorable, far beneath one such as him. For they prolonged it: kicking and punching and stabbing and slicing him just enough to keep him clinging to life. One of them even emptied his bladder, laughing as he washed away some of the blood.

But my brother didn't give up: he never stopped struggling, not even when the guts were spilling from his stomach.

Again and again the Crows come forward, grasping at Grace, pulling her into their pasts. And though she thrashes out, reeling from the horror of it, still they advance, determined that she should witness—that she should *feel*—what was done to them.

You have to live through it, Ellen had said.

And Grace knows now, why the Crows gather: they come to tell their story.

Over and over, they show her; the desecration of their town, the slaughter of their people. Sometimes two Crows grasp her at once, sometimes a Crow returns and she suffers the same scene twice, sometimes the vision is so clouded by terror it no longer holds meaning. But Grace relives it all anyway, every moment of their tale, until she is cowering against its assault, only able to decipher snatches of the pain and fear and anguish.

. . ."You must go!" he was screaming at me. "Run to the back gate, and don't look back—don't look back for anything!"

. . .I did not care what magic they yielded, I would tear off their limbs, I would strip the flesh from their bodies . . .

. . .I couldn't find my sister. While everything raged around me, she was all I could think of, but I didn't know where she'd gone . . .

. . . "There's no way out!" I shouted. "They're surrounding the wall!" . . .

. . . Blood, blood, there was so much blood. And I wanted it to stop, I wanted it all to end . . .

. . . "Mercy," we cried, "mercy!" . . .

. . . "Help us!" . . .

. . . "Please!" . . .

A long time later—a lifetime later—it stops. Grace is curled up in the dead earth, her head in her hands.

"I didn't know," she whispers. "Why did no one tell me?"

The largest Crow drifts forward once more, stopping just above her. With the little strength she has left, Grace turns her mud and tear-stained face towards it. Towards *him*, for she can almost see them now, the people who were torn from this place.

They kept me until last. I believe it was deliberate: they wanted me to see the blood-smeared streets, the smashed-up houses, the bodies piled in every corner; they wanted me to hear each scream, every plea for salvation; they wanted me to understand the extent of what I had done, in letting them in.

When all was quiet, the strangers dragged me back to the gate, where their leader forced me to my knees and addressed his men with words I didn't understand.

(But Grace understands).

"This land belongs to us now. We have cleared it of these creatures—of those Untamed by God—and now we will rebuild this as a holy place for our children, and for our children's children!"

I welcomed death then. As he put his knife against my throat, I closed my eyes and that blade became a small, cold hand, beckoning me into the afterlife.

Both the circle of Crows and the girl at its center are still.

"Why did no one tell me?" Grace asks again.

Because no one knows, she realizes. *For who would think to question the words of the Charter or the Songs of Crossing?*

Grace thinks she can see now, why the Scarecrows are taken: they are the price the town must pay for peace, and she hasn't the strength to fight it anymore. After all, a willing soul once a generation versus everything she now knows—it does not seem too bad a bargain. So instead of standing, instead of struggling, she starts to cry anew, her whole body shuddering with grief.

After a time, one of the Crows begins to sing. It is a strange humming sound that Grace thinks she is imagining at first, for in all but the memories they have been silent. But then she remembers: she has heard this tune before, just last night, from the lips of another Scarecrow.

Soon, other Crows join in, until the whole circle is united in the deep, mournful song. Grace's tears stop, and she closes her eyes, feeling the elegy resonate through the earth beneath her. It is both the saddest and most beautiful sound she has ever heard: it spills into her, seeping through the cracks the Crows have made until she is flooded with it.

The song has no words—and if it did she wouldn't have recognized them—but Grace understands its meaning.

They purged us from this place, sing the Crows, *and only the land remembers.*

The sky is lighter when Grace opens her eyes. She has been drifting, dreaming, but suddenly she jerks into a sitting position, staring around at the land, her heartbeat quickening. But there is nothing to see: all the Crows have gone.

A breathless laugh escapes her. *I am still here,* she thinks.

Their story, however, also remains. It returns to Grace now, and she is besieged again by the sights and sounds and smells of the massacre.

"Stop it!" she cries, though there is no one there to listen.

She shakes her head, as though she could dislodge that knowledge, as though all of it could somehow trickle away. She can still hear the song of the Crows, although perhaps it is she who is humming it. She tries to recall a hymn—any hymn—to distract herself, but cannot think of a single one.

Instead, she turns to focus on the dark outline of the town behind her. She is now free to return, but how can she go back? How can she walk through those streets, knowing what happened there?

"Why wasn't I taken?" she wonders aloud.

But even as she says it, she finds herself questioning whether *any* of the Scarecrows had been taken. All the Crows did to her was show what had been done to them. Did they really steal men and women from the land as payment, or were the Scarecrows who had disappeared actually the strong ones—the people who refused to go back, knowing what they knew?

"*. . . Can you promise me you'll return, no matter what happens with those—those creatures?*"

He is a good man, her father—her whole community is full of decent, virtuous people. Are they to blame, for what was done?

As questions chase one another through her mind, Grace clutches at her head, her nails digging into her scalp.

"Dear Heavenly God . . ." she begins instinctively, but can go no further, for the distant words of an executioner override her attempt at prayer.

"*This land belongs to us now. We have cleared it of these creatures—of those Untamed by God—and now we will rebuild this as a holy place for our children, and for our children's children!*"

Grace wails, pressing her knuckles into her temples, trying to make it stop. Her town, her history, her God: in giving her the truth, the Crows have taken away everything else.

What is it all for, then? What is the Scarecrow's fate? Is she supposed to go on as normal, never speak of what she knows, at the cost of her own sanity (. . . *some days she's better than others* . . .) or even her life (. . . *within a year he had hanged himself from the rafters of the town hall* . . .)? Is she meant to leave, turn her back on everything she knows, and pretend that it never happened, that the town doesn't even exist (. . . *William Bell survived, thirty years ago. I know he moved on, but by all accounts his farm prospers* . . .)? Or is she supposed to tell the truth; go back and rip apart the very foundations of her home? How would she even begin? And why should anyone believe her? (. . . *we all saw the state she was in—heard the wicked things she said* . . .)

Something flashes in the corner of her eye, something so bright Grace feels as though she's been stung. She cringes towards the ground, expecting some further ordeal, but then realizes the distant glare is the day's first glimpse of the sun.

After the horror of the night, it is an unexpected, almost overwhelming sight. Grace struggles to her feet, her body cold and stiff, and turns to face the sun head-on. She watches as light begins to stretch over the land, and with tears coursing down her cheeks once more, she raises her arms, waiting for the dawn's embrace. But it does not come: the sun cannot quite touch her, there in the blackened earth, just as it cannot reach the other places where the Crows have stood—those scars that tell of long-forgotten wounds.

If I Only Had an Autogenic Cognitive Decision Matrix

Scott Burtness

Clots of mud and foliage stained with dark vital-fluid marked Scarecrow's path from the airlock. Initiating a physical-assessment scan, it analyzed the extent of its injuries, categorizing them by degree of severity. Despite openly weeping vital fluid, none were terminal, nor were any severe enough to degrade its capabilities. Shifting its awareness, Scarecrow observed Jorry, the human wet-tech assigned as its Tin Man. The human's posture, facial expressions, and bio-signatures indicated that he also did not believe Scarecrow's wounds to be severe. Applying the relevant pre-loaded decision matrix, it determined that updating the Dorothy took precedence and established a communication link.

"Scarecrow to mining site." It formed the words slowly, hindered by facial muscles not well-shaped for Consortium Standard. "Mission accomplished."

"Roger, Scarecrow," the human female assigned as their unit's Dorothy acknowledged over the comm. "Tin Man, please verify."

Scarecrow noted that the audio quality of the com-link was slightly squelched, the result of atypically strong Van Allen belts in the heavy metals-rich moon. To facilitate optimal communication, it adjusted the audio controls as the human male spoke.

"Confirm mission accomplished," the wet-tech verified, running a hand through sweat-dampened hair. Sealing the airlock door and prepping for transit, he continued his update for the Dorothy's mission log. "Deterrence successful, Taboo Zone perimeter intact. Two crow fatalities, unprovoked and unavoidable. Scarecrow sustained injuries, but none of them seem severe. We're prepped for return. I'll initiate repairs in transit."

"Estimated time of arrival?" the Dorothy queried.

"Well, Genevieve, I'm glad you asked," the Tin Man replied. "Scarecrow, how long to base?"

Scarecrow considered variables, mentally calling up and discarding numerous potentialities that could affect travel time. "Transport will arrive at base in thirty-seven local minutes," it vocalized, watching closely for its Tin Man's reaction. The human smiled and engaged the transport's auto-navigation system. Applying a physiological-emotional reduction algorithm it had developed, Scarecrow cross-referenced the smile with its iconic database of two hundred and forty eight others from its Tin Man. Analysis indicated the human was pleased.

"Acknowledged," the Dorothy responded. "ETA thirty-seven local minutes. Full debrief scheduled for local eighteen-thirty. Mission log complete."

The near subsonic drone of anti-gravity cyclers spinning up introduced a dissonant chord to the otherwise quiet cabin. A moment later, the small craft rose from the forest floor and accelerated through the trees, accompanied by a soft hum. Coarse, dark leaves and thin, supple branches whispered along the transport's canopy as they passed.

The com-link chimed twice to signal that recording had stopped. Scarecrow was about to disconnect when the Dorothy spoke again.

"Jorry, would you care to explain why you're teaching the Scarecrow navigational computations?" the human female asked. "And more importantly, what happened out there? Data feed was showing a textbook perfect spook job."

The Tin Man placed a suture-stapler, antiseptic gel, and a heavy roll of synth-skin on a floating tray and motioned for Scarecrow to extend its right wing-analog. Scarecrow stretched the limb as directed, careful to avoid bumping the tray. Two and a half meters of corded muscle and functional joints unfolded, terminating in a tridactyl claw. The length of the limb was covered with black, overlapping, exocutaneous growths splayed like feathers. The growths covered Scarecrow's entire body except for the lower half of its thick legs and anisodactyl claws, which were wrapped in densely spaced, rigid scales.

Bioengineered to resemble the moon's indigenous sentient race, Scarecrow considered its appearance. The semblance of black feathers, clawed feet, and beaklike mouths gave rise to the "crow" moniker used by humans to describe the aliens. Any resemblance to the Corvidae family found on most Earth-derived planets ended there, however. Scarecrow's research had informed it that the crows of this moon shared no parallel evolutionary traits with any type of aviary-analog species catalogued by Consortium scientists.

Scarecrow also knew that, while similar, it was not typical of the indigenous species. The Dorothy's xenothropology team had discovered religious iconography depicting the crows' deity, and the wet-tech had designed Scarecrow accordingly. Standing over three meters tall and weighing about 300 kilograms, it stood a full meter and a half taller than the average adult crow.

Turning its head, Scarecrow inspected the jagged tear in the exocutaneous growths stretching along the ulna bone to its carpal joint. When the Tin Man picked up the suture-stapler, a memory of previous repairs surfaced. Analyzing the retrieved sensory data, it disabled its pain receptors and returned its attention to the conversing humans.

"Scare's learning navigational computations because he's really, really smart. To answer your other question, the problem could be that we're writing the damn textbook as we go," the Tin Man stated. "In a nutshell, Gen, the crows didn't spook. Scare went through the protocol script. Forbidden land, stay away, fire and brimstone, whatever. You definitely got the language right. The crows all quivered and kowtowed. Unfortunately, this time they didn't scatter."

The Tin Man started working his way around Scarecrow, suture-stapler clicking and hissing. Scarecrow registered an acrid smell as the hot sutures singed his torn flesh.

"While the rest were face-down in the dirt, one big warrior crow suddenly lunged, ripped out another crow's heart, and offered it up to Scare. The others started to scream, making this weird ululating sound that I've never heard before. Next thing you know, they're swaying back and forth, fanning their limbs while the big one held up the heart. Since that behavior wasn't defined in the event-response parameters, Scare didn't do anything. It just stood there. The big crow must've been offended, because it threw down the heart and attacked. When it was over, Scarecrow repeated the protocol script and the rest of the crows finally fled."

Scarecrow noticed tonal similarities between the Dorothy's slow exhalation and the sound of leaves across the canopy. It saved the comparison for future examination and continued listening. When the human female spoke, her words came faster than before.

"Jorry, that's amazing. We suspected they engaged in ritual sacrifice, but haven't had a chance to see it yet. You might have witnessed a genuine expiatory rite. Or not. It's possible that it didn't signify atonement. Do you think the sounds they were making were actually ululating, or could it have been more like singing, or praise? Were they distraught, or could it have been joy? I mean, they did just meet their god. Demonstrating worship and devotion with a physical offering of a heart is pretty consistent across xeno-cultures in early stage mythic-literal religious evolution."

The Dorothy exhaled again. Scarecrow noted the differences from her earlier sigh. Since its awakening in the vitrovat, it had collected one hundred and sixteen samples of contextual sighs from humans at the mining site. Each sample allowed it to refine its algorithms and extrapolate from a greater range of cognitive and emotional states as expressed by exhalations of breath. Scarecrow associated the Dorothy's first exhalation with anticipation and excitement, the latter with frustration or anxiety.

"Of course, it could also be a localized reaction to the Scarecrow," the Dorothy continued more slowly. "Maybe we've instigated a previously nonexistent religious ceremony. It's possible that the crows nearest to the Taboo Zone only started making sacrifices now that their god is showing up in the flesh."

"You're welcome," the Tin Man said.

"Jorry, this is serious. Consortium brass will be furious if they think we've artificially influenced the crows' social evolution. You know the rules. We have permission to get in, mine the metals, and get out, but there can be zero social-technological influence. No indigenous contact besides the Scarecrow. Even that is supposed to be as infrequent as possible, just enough to enforce the Taboo Zone and keep them away from the mine," the Dorothy said. "I'll need the holovid as soon as you're back so I can update the event-response parameters. If the Scarecrow gets caught up in a similar ritual, I wonder what the appropriate response should be."

"Beats me, Gen. You're the xeno-shrink. I'm just a wet-tech," the Tin Man commented while opening the package of synth-skin. "Maybe we could talk about it over dinner."

Scarecrow's sensitive olfactory passages noted an increase in pheromones from the human male. Intrigued by the event, it scanned a human reproductive biology file and determined it was ineffective for the human male to release a chemical signature when the human female was not in physical proximity. Also, there were no estrogen pheromones present that would have elicited a response from the human male's hypothalami. Scarecrow concluded that more data was required before it could start to assemble an appropriate situational-assessment algorithm. Shifting its bulk to allow the Tin Man easier access to a gash on the side of its torso, it continued to capture the unusual conversation for future review.

"Xenothropologist, not xeno-shrink," the Dorothy replied. "Cultural norms, social and religious development is plenty, thanks. Somebody else can figure out their individual psyches. And I'm not sure I want to discuss alien ritual sacrifice while eating."

"After dinner?" the Tin Man asked.

"Jorry . . ."

"Or after, after dinner, like after the barracks go lights-out," the Tin Man suggested.

The Dorothy spoke again, her voice echoing slightly as the com-link channel wavered.

"You're persistent, I'll give you that. But no, Jorry. Look, you know the rules about fraternizing on assignment."

The Tin Man stopped mid-stitch. "So you're saying if we weren't on assignment . . . ?"

"Jorry, enough," the Dorothy replied. "Just get me that holovid as soon as you dock." A sudden, two-toned chime indicated a terminated com-link.

The Tin Man dropped his head.

"I thought girls liked flowers," he grumbled. Looking up, he pointed a finger at Scarecrow's three eyes.

"You should talk to her more," the human suggested before returning to the sutures. "Your lexicon is the most expansive of any A.I. I've worked on, and that would definitely impress her."

"The mission outcome was conveyed," the Scarecrow stated, eliciting a short laugh from its Tin Man.

"Sure it was, and nicely done, too. 'Mission accomplished.' Beautifully descriptive, despite its brevity." Finishing the final sutures, the human swabbed on antiseptic gel, stretched lengths of synth-skin over Scarecrow's wounds and surveyed his work.

"Gen thinks A.I.'s could never deviate from core-purpose parameters," the Tin Man explained. "If you chatted her up, actually engaged her in autonomous non-mission dialogue, she'd see that crows aren't the only interesting, intelligent lifeform on this moon." Repairs finished, the human anchored the tray and returned its contents to the med-locker.

Scarecrow asked for clarification, turning its head to watch the Tin Man remove his fluid-stained coveralls and place them in the transport's recycler.

"Your enhancements. The cognitive psychology templates, self-generating sub-databases, seed algorithms, and ad hoc decision matrices. You're my grand experiment, Scarecrow," the Tin Man said. "Remember when I showed you the *Wizard of Oz*?"

Scarecrow nodded. "Earth Prime holovid. Fiction. Inspiration for occupational designations Dorothy, Tin Man, Scarecrow," it said in response, indicating the transport's com-speaker, the Tin Man's chest, and its own torso in sequence.

"Well, there's a bit more to it than that." For a moment, the wet-tech was occupied with documenting his repairs and updating the med-locker inventory. Turning back to face Scarecrow, he pointed with his stylus.

"Let's just say I'm trying to help you get a brain because I'm in search of a heart."

"Query. Why does Tin Man require additional chambered muscular organ? Is original unit deficient or impairing operational effectiveness?"

The human shook his head. "Looks like we need to work on your figurative-literal conversions." Jorry looked at Scarecrow from his chair. "Consider the crow ritual you experienced. It wasn't giving you a heart because it thought yours was in disrepair. A heart is also symbolic. To have someone's heart is to have their devotion, their love." When Scarecrow didn't respond, the human continued.

"After we debrief, I'll schedule a programming session on similes, analogies, metaphors, and idioms. That should help inform your contextual interpretation algorithms. Go ahead and store this conversation so we can reference it later," the Tin Man instructed, returning his attention to his notes.

Rather than storing the conversation for future review, Scarecrow kept it active for immediate contemplation. As they traversed the moon's forest toward the mine site, Scarecrow sat quietly, considering what it had learned.

After precisely thirty-seven local minutes of travel time, Scarecrow watched a large slab of natural stone shudder as servo-pistons pushed and lifted it away from the surrounding mountainside. Sliding on pneumonic gliders, it moved sideways, opening a previously hidden tunnel. Scarecrow listened to the anti-gravity cyclers wind down as the transport slowed and came to a stop. The Tin Man tripped the airlock and stepped down to the transport bay's floor. Scarecrow exited more slowly, bending slightly to accommodate the airlock's size.

Despite the muted sounds of the mining operations, Scarecrow felt the ever-present vibrations beneath its clawed feet as it followed the Tin Man to where the Dorothy was waiting. Recalling its Tin Man's earlier recommendation, it formulated a statement.

"Hello Genevieve," Scarecrow vocalized. "Scarecrow will learn figurative-literal conversion following debrief."

The human female turned toward Scarecrow, facial expression altering as she reacted to its self-initiated dialogue. Shifting its awareness to the human male, Scarecrow noted the widening smile on its Tin Man's face. Analysis of the smile indicating that its cognitive actions were in conformance with the Tin Man's objectives, Scarecrow enabled a newly developed, autogenic decision matrix. Stepping forward, it extended a limb and grasped the Dorothy's shoulder. Applying pressure to immobilize her, Scarecrow thrust its other claw forward, piercing the female human's chest. Expanding its digits, it snapped the breastbone and wrenched open her ribcage, allowing Scarecrow to completely encase the small heart in its grip. A sharp twist, and the tissue anchoring the chambered organ within the chest cavity tore free.

As the Tin Man screamed his joy, Scarecrow captured the event-response, validated the preceding logic chain, and offered up the Dorothy's devotion and love.

CONTRIBUTORS

Andrew Bud Adams was raised by spider-men and turtle ninjas and *ronin* rabbits, who are now helping raise his own children. "The Straw Samurai," inspired by them and the Japanese folk tale "The Tengu's Magic Cloak," is one of his first published retellings. When not wandering between fantasy villages or teaching college writing, he can be found on Twitter @andrewbudadams.

Whenever grownups asked young **Laura Blackwood** what she wanted to be when she grew up, she said "Published!" That dream finally came true—"Black Birds" is her first story to see print. Laura currently lives and works in Edmonton, Alberta, and tinkers with many more writing projects than is considered wise or healthy.

Amanda Block is a writer and ghostwriter based in Edinburgh, UK. A graduate of the Creative Writing Masters at the University of Edinburgh, she is often inspired by myths and fairy tales, frequently using them as a starting point to tell other stories. Amanda's work has been featured in anthologies such as *Modern Grimmoire, Stories for Homes,* and World Weaver Press' *Fae.* She has been shortlisted for the Bridport Prize and the Chapter One Promotions Short Story Competition. Amanda is currently working on her first novel. She can be found online at amandawritersblock.blogspot.co.uk.

Scott Burtness lives in Minnesota with his wife, Liz and their English Staffordshire-Boxer, Frank. He has it on good authority that he possesses all of the requisite parts to be considered human, and sincerely believes he's taller when measured with the metric system. Scott's debut novel, WISCONSIN VAMP, is available now. When not writing horror-comedy romps or sci-fi adventures, Scott enjoys bowling, karaoke, craft brews and afternoon naps. Follow him on Twitter (@SWBauthor). Don't follow him down dark alleys.

Virginia Carraway Stark started her writing career with three successful screenplays and went on to write speculative fiction as well as writing plays and for various blogs. She has written for several anthologies and three novels as well. Her novel, *Dalton's Daughter* is available now through Amazon and Starlight Press. *Detachment's Daughter* and *Carnival Fun* are coming later this year. You can find her on Twitter @tweetsbyvc, and on Facebook Facebook.com/virginiacarrawaystark.

Amanda C. Davis has an engineering degree and a fondness for baking, gardening, and low-budget horror films. Her work has appeared in *Crossed Genres, InterGalactic Medicine Show*, and others. She tweets enthusiastically as @davisac1. You can find out more about her and read more of her work at amandacdavis.com. Her collection of retold fairy tales with Megan Engelhardt, *Wolves and Witches*, is available from World Weaver Press.

Megan Fennell is a court clerk, cat owner, and writer of strange tales, currently living and working in Lethbridge, Alberta. Although loving magpies to the point of having two of them tattooed on her, it was the Danish myth of the Valravn that held her corvid-like attention span for this anthology. Her stories can also be found in *Wrestling with Gods: Tesseracts 18, Tesseracts 17, OnSpec Magazine*, and the charity anthology *Help: Twelve Tales of Healing*.

Kim Goldberg is an award-winning writer and author of six books. She is a winner of the Rannu Fund Poetry Prize for Speculative Literature and other distinctions. Her speculative tales and poems have appeared in numerous magazines and anthologies including *Tesseracts 11, Zahir Tales, On Spec, Urban Green Man, Dark Mountain, Imaginarium, Here Be Monsters, Switched On Gutenberg* and elsewhere. Her seventh book, *Refugium*, about people living with electrosensitivity, will be released in 2015. She lives in Nanaimo, BC, and online at PigSquashPress.com.

Katherine Marzinsky is a writer and student currently residing in New Jersey. She attends Kean University, where she is working toward an undergraduate degree with a major in English and a minor in Spanish. Her previous work has appeared in *Asimov's Science Fiction Magazine, A Cappella Zoo, Cease, Cows,* and *The Inanimates I* story anthology.

Craig Pay is a short story author and novelist. He writes speculative fiction (usually). His short stories have appeared with a number of different magazines and anthologies. He is represented by John Jarrold. Craig runs the successful Manchester Speculative Fiction writers' group. He enjoys Chinese martial arts and many other hobbies. You can visit him at craigpay.com.

Sara Puls spends most of her time lawyering, researching, writing, and editing. Her dreams frequently involve strange mash-ups of typography, fairy creatures, courtrooms, and blood. Sara's stories have been published in *Daily Science Fiction, The Future Fire, GigaNotoSaurus, Penumbra*, World Weaver Press's *Fae* anthology, and elsewhere. She also co-edits *Scigentasy*, a gender- and identity-focused spec fic zine. On Twitter, she is @sarapuls.

Holly Schofield's work has appeared in many publications including *Lightspeed, Crossed Genres,* and *Tesseracts*. For more of her work, see hollyschofield.wordpress.com.

Laura VanArendonk Baugh was born at a very early age and never looked back. She overcame childhood deficiencies of having been born without teeth or developed motor skills, and by the time she matured into a recognizable adult she had become a behavior analyst, an internationally-recognized animal trainer, a costumer/cosplayer, a dark chocolate addict, and a Pushcart Prize-nominated author with a following for her folklore-based stories and speculative fiction. Find her at LauraVanArendonkBaugh.com.

Kristina Wojtaszek grew up as a woodland sprite and mermaid, playing around the shores of Lake Michigan. At any given time she could be found with live snakes tangled in her hair and worn out shoes filled with sand. She earned a bachelor's degree in Wildlife Management as an excuse to spend her days lost in the woods with a book in hand. Now a mother of two little tricksters and their menagerie of small beasts, she continues to conjure bits of fantasy during the rare spell of silence. Her fairy tales, ghost stories, poems and YA fiction have been published by World Weaver Press (*Opal, Fae, and Specter Spectacular*), *Far Off Places* and *Sucker Literary Magazine*. Follow her @KristinaWojtasz or on her blog, Twice Upon a Time.

Jane Yolen, often called "the Hans Christian Andersen of America"(*Newsweek*) is the author of well over 350 books, including OWL MOON, THE DEVIL'S ARITHMETIC, and HOW DO DINOSAURS SAY GOODNIGHT. Her books and stories have won an assortment of awards—two Nebulas, a World Fantasy Award, a Caldecott, the Golden Kite Award, three Mythopoeic awards, two Christopher Medals, a nomination for the National Book Award, and the Jewish Book Award, among many others. She has been nominated three times for the Pushcart Prize in Poetry. She is also the winner (for body of work) of the World Fantasy Assn. Lifetime Achievement Award, Science Fiction Poetry Association Grand Master Award, Catholic Library's Regina Medal, Kerlan Medal from the University of

Minnesota, the du Grummond Medal from Un. of Southern Missisippi, the Smith College Alumnae Medal, and New England Pubic Radio Arts and Humanities Award . Six colleges and universities have given her honorary doctorates. Her website is: www.janeyolen.com.

∽

ABOUT THE ANTHOLOGIST

Rhonda Parrish is driven by a desire to do All The Things. She has been the publisher and editor-in-chief of *Niteblade Magazine* for nearly eight years now (which is like *forever* in internet time) and is the editor of several anthologies including *Fae* and *B is for Broken*. In addition, Rhonda is a writer whose work has been in dozens of publications like *Tesseracts 17: Speculating Canada from Coast to Coast, Imaginarium: The Best Canadian Speculative Writing* (2012) and *Mythic Delirium*. Her website, updated weekly, is at rhondaparrish.com.

FORTHCOMING ANTHOLOGIES IN THE SERIES RHONDA PARRISH'S MAGICAL MENAGERIES

The anthologies **Fae**, **Corvidae** and **Scarecrow** are available in ebook and paperback. Turn the page for more information about these works.

August 15 – December 15, 2015, Rhonda Parrish will be reading for **Sirens,** a new anthologies in the same series, to be published in 2016. More information at WorldWeaverPress.com.

CORVIADE

anthology

Rhonda Parrish's Magical Menageries

A flock of shiny stories! Associated with life and death, disease and luck, corvids have long captured mankind's attention, showing up in mythology as the companions or manifestations of deities, and starring in stories from Aesop to Poe and beyond.

In Corvidae birds are born of blood and pain, trickster ravens live up to their names, magpies take human form, blue jays battle evil forces, and choughs become prisoners of war. These stories will take you to the Great War, research facilities, frozen mountaintops, steam-powered worlds, remote forest homes, and deep into fairy tales. One thing is for certain, after reading this anthology, you'll never look the same way at the corvid outside your window.

Featuring works by Jane Yolen, Mike Allen, C.S.E. Cooney, M.L.D. Curelas, Tim Deal, Megan Engelhardt, Megan Fennell, Adria Laycraft, Kat Otis, Michael S. Pack, Sara Puls, Michael M. Rader, Mark Rapacz, Angela Slatter, Laura VanArendonk Baugh, and Leslie Van Zwol.

❧

Available now in ebook and trade paperback.

FAE

anthology
Rhonda Parrish's Magical Menageries

Meet Robin Goodfellow as you've never seen him before, watch damsels in distress rescue themselves, get swept away with the selkies and enjoy tales of hobs, green men, pixies and phookas. One thing is for certain, these are not your grandmother's fairy tales.

Fairies have been both mischievous and malignant creatures throughout history. They've dwelt in forests, collected teeth or crafted shoes. Fae is full of stories that honor that rich history while exploring new and interesting takes on the fair folk from castles to computer technologies and modern midwifing, the Old World to Indianapolis.

With an introduction by Sara Cleto and Brittany Warman, and all new stories from Sidney Blaylock Jr., Amanda Block, Kari Castor, Beth Cato, Liz Colter, Rhonda Eikamp, Lor Graham, Alexis A. Hunter, L.S. Johnson, Jon Arthur Kitson, Adria Laycraft, Lauren Liebowitz, Christine Morgan, Shannon Phillips, Sara Puls, Laura VanArendonk Baugh, and Kristina Wojtaszek.

Available now in ebook and trade paperback.

ALSO BY SCARECROW CONTRIBUTORS

White as snow, stained with blood,
her talons black as ebony . . .

OPAL
a novella by
Kristina Wojtaszek

"A fairy tale within a fairy tale
within a fairy tale—the narratives fit together
like interlocking pieces of a puzzle,
beautifully told."
—Zachary Petit, Editor *Writer's Digest*

In this retwisting of the classic Snow White tale, the daughter of an owl is forced into human shape by a wizard who's come to guide her from her wintry tundra home down to the colorful world of men and Fae, and the father she's never known. She struggles with her human shape and grieves for her dead mother—a mother whose past she must unravel if men and Fae are to live peacefully together.

"Twists and turns and surprises that kept me up well into the night. Fantasy and fairy tale lovers will eat this up and be left wanting more!"
—Kate Wolford, Editor, *Enchanted Conversation Magazine*

Available now in ebook and trade paperback.

ALSO BY SCARECROW CONTRIBUTORS

WOLVES AND WITCHES
A Fairy Tale Collection
Amanda C. Davis and Megan Engelhardt

Witches have stories too. So do mermaids, millers' daughters, princes (charming or otherwise), even big bad wolves. They may be a bit darker–fewer enchanted ball gowns, more iron shoes. Happily-ever-after? Depends on who you ask. In *Wolves and Witches*, sisters Amanda C. Davis and Megan Engelhardt weave sixteen stories and poems out of familiar fairy tales, letting them show their teeth.

"I made the mistake of starting it late one evening and couldn't go to sleep until I had read it all. With their dark prose and evocative poetry these sisters have done the Brothers Grimm proud."
— Rhonda Parrish, *Niteblade Fantasy and Horror Magazine* and editor of *Scarecrow* and *Corvidae*

"Dark and delicious revenge-filled tales! I Highly Recommend this fun and small collection of short stories."
— Fangs, Wands & Fairy Dust.

"Sisters Amanda C. Davis and Megan Engelhardt are the female Brothers Grimm."
— K. Allen Wood, *Shock Totem*

Available now in ebook and trade paperback.

MORE GREAT SHORT FICTION

Far Orbit: Speculative Space Adventures
Science fiction in the Grand Tradition—Anthology
Edited by Bascomb James

The King of Ash and Bones
Breathtaking four-story collection
Rebecca Roland

Krampusnacht: Twelve Nights of Krampus
A Christmas Krampus Anthology
Edited by Kate Wolford

Wolves and Witches
A Fairy Tale Collection
Witches have stories too. So do mermaids, millers' daughters, princes (charming or otherwise), even big bad wolves.
Amanda C. Davis and Megan Engelhardt

Cursed: Wickedly Fun Stories
Collection
"Quirky, clever, and just a little savage." —Lane Robins, critically acclaimed author of MALEDICTE and KINGS AND ASSASSINS
Susan Abel Sullivan

BEYOND THE GLASS SLIPPER
TEN NEGLECTED FAIRY TALES TO FALL IN LOVE WITH

Introduction and Annotations by Kate Wolford

Some fairy tales everyone knows—these aren't those tales. These are tales of kings who get deposed and pigs who get married. These are ten tales, much neglected. Editor of *Enchanted Conversation: A Fairy Tale Magazine*, Kate Wolford, introduces and annotates each tale in a manner that won't leave novices of fairy tale studies lost in the woods to grandmother's house, yet with a depth of research and a delight in posing intriguing puzzles that will cause folklorists and savvy readers to find this collection a delicious new delicacy.

Beyond the Glass Slipper is about more than just reading fairy tales—it's about connecting to them. It's about thinking of the fairy tale as a precursor to *Saturday Night Live* as much as it is to any princess-movie franchise: the tales within these pages abound with outrageous spectacle and absurdist vignettes, ripe with humor that pokes fun at ourselves and our society.

Never stuffy or pedantic, Kate Wolford proves she's the college professor you always wish you had: smart, nurturing, and plugged into pop culture. Wolford invites us into a discussion of how these tales fit into our modern cinematic lives and connect the larger body of fairy tales, then asks—no, *insists*—that we create our own theories and connections. A thinking man's first step into an ocean of little known folklore.

Available now in ebook and trade paperback.

SHARDS OF HISTORY

first in a fantasy series
Rebecca Roland

"A must for any fantasy reader."
—*Plasma Frequency Magazine*

Feared and reviled, the fierce, winged creatures known as Jeguduns live in the cliffs surrounding the Taakwa valley. When Malia discovers an injured Jegudun in the valley, she risks everything—exile from the village, loss of her status as clan mother in training, even her life—to befriend and save the surprisingly intelligent creature. But all of that pales when she learns the truth: the threat to her people is bigger and more malicious than the Jeguduns. Lurking on the edge of the valley is an Outsider army seeking to plunder and destroy her people. It's only a matter of time before the Outsiders find a way through the magic that protects the valley—a magic that can only be created by Taakwa and Jeguduns working together.

"Fast-paced, high-stakes drama in a fresh fantasy world. Rebecca Roland is a newcomer to watch!"
  —James Maxey, author of *Greatshadow: The Dragon Apocalypse.*

"One of the most beautifully written novels I have ever read. Suspenseful, entrapping, and simply . . . well, let's just say that *Shards of History* reminds us of why we love books in the first place. *Five out of five stars!*"
  —Good Choice Reading

Available now in ebook and trade paperback

FAR ORBIT

Speculative Space Adventures—Anthology
Edited by Bascomb James

*Modern space adventures crafted by a new generation
of Grand Tradition science fiction writers.*

Smart and engaging stories that take us back to a time when science fiction was fun and informative, pithy and piquant—when speculative fiction transported us from the everyday grind and left us wondrously satisfied. Showcasing the breadth of Grand Tradition stories, from 1940s-style pulp to realistic hard SF, from noir and horror SF to spaceships, alien uplift, and action-adventure motifs, Far Orbit's diversity of Grand Tradition stories makes it easy for every SF fan to find a favorite.

Featuring an open letter to SF by Elizabeth Bear and stories from Gregory Benford, Tracy Canfield, Eric Choi, Barbara Davies, Jakob Drud, Julie Frost, David Wesley Hill, K. G. Jewell, Sam Kepfield, Kat Otis, Jonathan Shipley, Wendy Sparrow, and Peter Wood

"Daring adventure, protagonists who think on their feet, and out of this world excitement! Welcome to FAR ORBIT, a fine collection of stories in the best SF tradition. Strap in and enjoy!"
—Julie E. Czerneda, author of SPECIES IMPERATIVE

"Successfully captures the kinds of stories that were the gateway drugs for many of us who have been reading science fiction for a long time. Well done!"
—Tangent

Available now in ebook and trade paperback.

THE DEVIL IN MIDWINTER

Paranormal romance (NA)

Elise Forier Edie

A handsome stranger, a terrifying monster,
a boy who burns and burns . . .

Mattawa, Washington, is usually a sleepy orchard town come December, until a murder, sightings of a fantastic beast, and the arrival of a handsome new vintner in town kindle twenty-year-old reporter Esme Ulloa's curiosity—and maybe her passion as well. But the more she untangles the mystery, the more the world Esme knows unspools, until she finds herself navigating a place she thought existed only in storybooks, where dreams come alive, monsters walk the earth and magic is real. When tragedy strikes close to home, Esme finds she must strike back, matching wits with an ancient demon in a deadly game, where everything she values stands to be lost, including the love of her life.

Night Owl Reviews top pick!

Available now in ebook and trade paperback.

ALSO FROM WORLD WEAVER PRESS

Far Orbit: Speculative Space Adventures
Science fiction in the Grand Traditon—Anthology
Edited by Bascomb James

The Haunted Housewives of Allister, Alabama
Cleo Tidwell Paranormal Mystery, Book One
Who knew one gaudy Velvet Elvis
could lead to such a heap of haunted trouble?
Susan Abel Sullivan

The Weredog Whisperer
Cleo Tidwell Paranormal Mystery, Book Two
The Tidwells are supposed to be on spring break on the Florida Gulf Coast,
not up to their eyeballs in paranormal hijinks . . . again
Susan Abel Sullivan

Heir to the Lamp
Genie Chronicles, Book One (YA)
A family secret, a mysterious lamp, a dangerous Order with the mad desire
to possess both
Michelle Lowery combs

Legally Undead
Vampirachy, Book One
A reluctant vampire hunter, stalking New York City
as only a scorned bride can.
Margo Bond Collins

Glamour
Stealing the life she's always wanted is as easy as casting a spell (YA)
Andrea Janes

Blood Chimera
Blood Chimera Paranormal Mystery, Book One
Some ransoms aren't meant to be paid
Jenn Lyons

Blood Sin
Blood Chimera Paranormal Mystery, Book Two
Everything is permitted . . . and everyone has their price
Jenn Lyons

Specter Spectacular: 13 Ghostly Tales
Anthology
Once you cross the grave into this world of fantasy and fright, you may find there's no way back
Edited by Eileen Wiedbrauk

A Winter's Enchantment
Three novellas of winter magic and loves lost and regained
Experience the magic of the season
Elise Forier Edie, Amalia Dillin, Kristina Wojatszek

❧

For more on these and other titles visit
WorldWeaverPress.com.

WORLD WEAVER PRESS

Publishing fantasy, paranormal, and science fiction.
We believe in great storytelling.

Made in the USA
Charleston, SC
05 August 2015